Anne Boleyn and Me

My Story.

Anne Boleyn and Me

The Diary of
Elinor Valjean, London 1525-1536

By Alison Prince

While the events described and some of the characters in this book may be based on actual historical events and real people, Elinor Valjean is a fictional character, created by the author, and her diary is a work of fiction.

This edition produced for the Book People Ltd,
Hall Wood Avenue, Haydock, St Helens WA11 9UL

First published in the UK by Scholastic Ltd, 2004

Text copyright © Alison Prince, 2004

ISBN 0 439 95492 4

All rights reserved
Printed and bound by Nørhaven Paperback A/S, Denmark
Cover image: Self portrait by Anguiscola: Private Collection, Milan,
Italy/Bridgeman Art Library
Background image: Hampton Court Quad: Private Collection/The Stapleton
Collection/Bridgeman Art Library

The right of Alison Prince to be identified as the author of
this work has been asserted by her in accordance with the
Copyright, Designs and Patents Act, 1988.

Richmond Palace, 1525

13th August 1525

This is the diary of Elinor Valjean, aged eleven.

Today is my sister Rosanna's birthday. Mama gave her a beautiful diary to write in, because Rosanna is sixteen, the same age as Mama was when she came to England with Catherine of Aragon, our queen. I am going to write a diary as well, only I do not have a proper one, so I have to write it on scraps of paper. I will keep them in the back of my Latin book, so they will be private.

I am not jealous of Rosanna. Of course she must have nice things for her birthday. I gave her a beaded cap that I'd sewn myself, with some help from Mama. But I will have to wait a long time before I am sixteen, and I want to start writing my diary now. Mama began hers because she was leaving Spain and going on a dangerous sea voyage to a strange country. She showed Rosanna and me her diary, with its close-packed lines of neat Spanish writing. Mine will not look like that. I keep trying to make my writing smaller and more tidy, but I never seem to manage it.

Papa would laugh if he knew about my diary pages. He isn't unkind, but he laughs at everything. I suppose it is because he is the court jester, "Mr John", as they call him. He says he has to remember that things are funny because if he starts to think they are serious or sad, he would lose his job. I want to be a jester, too, but I am a girl, so I have to wear long dresses that make it hard to jump and tumble as he does. I wish I had been a boy. My brothers have far more fun, learning archery and fighting with swords and quarter-staves. Little William is not much good at it yet, being only four and not very strong, but Daniel, at seven, thinks himself quite the man.

Mama reminds me that I am lucky. She and Queen Catherine were childhood friends, so we live as members of the royal court, in whichever palace King Henry VIII chooses to have his household. Mama and Papa both serve the King and Queen, he as the jester and she as Catherine's friend and favourite lady, and we children will be royal servants when we are old enough. Meanwhile, we ourselves are served by a great army of people who work in the barns and the yards and the smoky kitchens, tending livestock, washing clothes, and preparing and serving food.

Yes, we are lucky. We do not put in long hours of

work in the fields, digging and sowing and reaping. We do not cart dung or pick stones or undertake the horrible work of slaughtering and skinning and plucking. Our food arrives ready-cooked, served on gold dishes if the King is entertaining guests. We play music and sing and dance, and every summer we go with the royal party on progress to other parts of the country while the palace where we have spent the winter is cleaned. When we come back in the autumn, we find the soot gone from the walls and the grease and filth scrubbed off the floors. There are fresh rushes scattered in the dining hall, sweet to tread on, and the bed-linen is washed and aired. I always love those first weeks after our return, while all the rooms still smell clean.

I would not have chosen to be a girl, but I enjoy some very nice things that the boys do not share. Sometimes Mama lets me join her when she and Maria de Salinas spend afternoons with the Queen. They talk together in Spanish, which I understand though I am not good at writing it, and they do their fine embroidery. Mostly it is Spanish style, black on white, as richly patterned as the bright sparkle of sunshine through dark leaves. It is very beautiful, but secretly I prefer the English use of reds and purples, blues and browns and gold. The Queen has all these colours, though she seldom uses them, and I love arranging the hanks of silk like a rainbow in their lacquered box. Queen Catherine said I could. She is a wonderful lady. Although she is the Queen of England, she is so kind.

I wish I was better at embroidery. I try hard, but my fingers seem sticky and awkward, and the thread makes itself into grubby knots. Perhaps I will find it easier when I am older. Meanwhile, I am always glad if Papa comes to join us, playing his lute or viol for the Queen and telling funny rhymes, for then I can lay the work down and listen. He can only be with us if King Henry does not need his services, for, like everyone else in the court, he has to obey orders.

This morning he could not come. To my amazement, Queen Catherine asked me to play instead, and handed me her own lute. I was very nervous, but she smiled, and when I had finished she clapped her hands. Papa must have told her I can dance as well, and that I make up my own stories, for she asked me to do these things, and afterwards she laughed and applauded again. She said I take after my father.

It was the greatest compliment she could pay me, for I would love to be like him. My brother Daniel would laugh if he knew I wanted to be a jester, and little William would laugh as well without understanding why. Even Mama and Rosanna might be shocked, so I never mention it. But I dream of it all the same, and then I feel warm and excited inside.

I must be careful not to get married, or I will never do anything but work as a wife and mother. Some girls have their first baby when they are only twelve, specially if they belong to the titled families. They could never be jesters, poor things.

Princesses have no say in choosing their husbands. The Queen's daughter, Princess Mary, is nine years old, two years younger than I am, but she was betrothed when she was six to the Holy Roman Emperor Charles V, who is a grown-up man. He is the Queen's nephew, so I should not be rude about him – but he is such a funny-looking person. I saw him when he came here for the betrothal ceremony, and he has a long, pointed chin that sticks out so he can hardly close his mouth. He belongs to the Habsburg family, and Mama says all of them look rather like that. Mary was sent off to Ludlow Castle last month, with a huge retinue of horses and servants, to live in a separate household there. I don't know why.

I must stop writing now. Mama is calling. She wants me to get William ready for bed. I tell him a story every night, and he will not go to sleep without it.

14th August 1525

Rosanna told me why Princess Mary went to live in Ludlow Castle. It's all to do with the King's son, Henry Fitzroy. He is six years old, and his mother is not Queen Catherine, she is called Bessie Blount. The little boy was brought here to Richmond Palace in June, and there was a big ceremony while the King made him Duke of Richmond and Somerset. Then he was sent to the north of England to be head of a great household. Rosanna says the Queen was annoyed because her own daughter, Mary, had not been given any such honours, and she told Henry she was not pleased. In fact, there was a frightful argument between them. So Mary has now been given her own household, to be equal with her half-brother.

I hope she will like it. I would hate to be sent away from my home and family to a castle near Wales, which they say is a very wet place. Thank goodness I am not a princess.

I saw Mark Smeaton catch Rosanna by her waist yesterday and give her a kiss. She was very offended and pushed him away. Mark said he was only trying to wish her a happy birthday, but I don't think she believed it. Mark is one of the court musicians. He plays the lute well and has a good voice, but Rosanna detests him. "He is pathetic," she said. "Like a trodden-on spaniel, always hoping people will like him. He has no spirit. He is just cheeky, and that is a different thing." I didn't understand what she meant. I quite like Mark. He gave me a bit of sugar candy the other day.

The King was in high good humour this morning. I saw him run his hand down Anne Boleyn's back as she went through a door ahead of him yesterday, then he laughed and bent his head to kiss her on the cheek. Anne works with Mama and Rosanna as one of the Queen's ladies, but she does not seem to mind being kissed. She smiled up at the King, all gaiety. She has been away at Hever Castle, her parents' home, for the last two years, and only came back quite recently. Rosanna says the King himself is in love with her, and he sent her away because she was having an affair with a young man called Henry Percy. There was quite a rumpus about it, and Cardinal Wolsey, the King's close adviser, told Percy that Anne Boleyn was not a suitable wife for a young man of good family. Percy was sent off to marry someone else. And Rosanna says Thomas Wyatt, the poet, is in love with Anne now.

I think all that is very silly. I love my family and I love the grey cat called Minna and the dogs that lie around when we all eat in the great hall, waiting for bones and scraps to be thrown. I love horses, too. But poets and young men called Percy sound a terrible bore.

This afternoon the King's mood changed completely, and he flew into one of his rages. Papa had a terrible time with him. King Henry loves music and plays well himself, so he is usually easy to amuse, but today something had upset him. Papa found out later that the Emperor Charles has broken off his engagement to Mary. The King has taken it as a personal insult, so his temper has been explosive ever since the news came. The whole court was tiptoeing about for fear of being shouted at, and even the Queen, who is always so calm and wise, dissolved into tears.

2nd October 1525

I meant to write my diary every day, but there are so many other things to do. I practise my dancing and singing, and Papa has given me a wooden flute, so that is a new instrument to learn, as well as the viol and lute. But I love the sound it makes, and Papa is a good teacher. My fingers are getting quicker at finding the notes.

Mark Smeaton still pesters Rosanna, though she won't have anything to do with him, and Thomas Wyatt gazes with soulful eyes at Anne Boleyn. But so does the King, which I find very odd. If she is too common a girl for young Percy to marry, how can she cast her spell on the King of England? Everyone is whispering that he is in love with her, but I can't understand it. King Henry is married to Queen Catherine, so how can he be in love with Anne? I am sure the Queen must be very upset about it. I asked Mama, and she sighed and said, "Poor lady – if only she had given him a son."

It is true that the Queen was unlucky. She had child after child, but all of them died except Mary. I know babies die sometimes. Mama had a little boy after I was born, and he died before he was a year old. But at least she has four of us. People say the Queen's last childbirth left her injured, so she cannot have any more children. The King is disappointed because he wanted a son who would inherit the throne of England. All this fuss about sons puzzles me. Surely Princess Mary can be Queen of England when King Henry dies? Her grandmother, Isabella, was Queen of Spain, and she ruled the country, with some help from her husband. If Isabella could do it, why not Mary? Mama shook her head when I suggested this. "King Henry is set on having a son," she said.

15th February 1526

There was a joust this afternoon. We watched from the covered stand, and Daniel was grumbling that he is not old enough yet to take part. I said, "But you will one day." He is lucky. I myself will always be sitting on the benches under the striped awning, a mere spectator.

When the men rode in, they looked magnificent, as they always do. They were in armour, of course, but scarlet plumes flew from their helmets, and they wore full-skirted, embroidered tunics. Their horses were beautifully dressed as well, in embroidered trappings that covered them almost completely, just showing the lower part of their legs. There was one I specially liked, in pale blue and silver.

When the King came riding in on his big, black horse, a murmur went up because his tunic was stitched with the words, DECLARE I DARE NOT. All the ladies were giggling behind their hands, and I asked Mama what it meant. Her face had turned quite pink and she said, "Never mind," so I asked Rosanna later. She told me the words meant the King has a new love, but he dares not say her name. But everyone knows her name. It is Anne Boleyn.

I keep thinking about Anne, wondering what it must be like to be loved by a king who already has a wife. I came face to face with her this evening as she brought a flask of sweet wine to the Queen's chamber. She is hardly taller than I am, a slender wisp of a thing. I suppose I must have been staring because she asked me what I thought I was looking at. She sounded very annoyed. It was no use pretending I hadn't been looking. I dropped her a respectful curtsey while I thought fast, then said, "I was looking at you."

"And why, pray?" she asked.

I told her, "Because you are so beautiful." Papa has always said a jester must look innocent.

It worked very well. "Bless the child," Anne said. She patted my cheek and smiled at me. Then she went on to the Queen's door with her flask of wine.

She is not really beautiful. She has a slim figure, but her face is very pale, with a pointed chin. Rosanna says she is quick-witted, with a ready retort to any courtier who makes a flirtatious remark, and the men like her for that. She has jet-black eyes, as lively as a bird's. She makes me think of a magpie; neat and smart and attracted to things that glitter. And I suppose the greatest and most glittering prize of them all must be the King.

19th April 1526

King Henry hurled a jug of wine at Papa today, causing him a deep cut above the eyebrow. Mama said nothing, just bathed the wound and put some knitbone ointment on it. This afternoon we heard that Henry has sent Thomas Wyatt away to Italy on some sort of diplomatic mission that will last for years. Rosanna laughed and said, "His Majesty must be getting desperate. He is not used to having his wishes refused."

Mama looked at her and shook her head. Neither of them would explain what Rosanna meant. But I met Mark Smeaton coming from the Queen's chamber with his lute, and I asked him. He was happy to tell me. "The King wants Anne to be his mistress, and she has turned him down. So he is raging about like a mad bull."

I know what a mistress is. It is a woman who lives with a man as if the pair of them were married, only they are not. I am glad Anne has refused to do that. It would be dreadful for Queen Catherine.

Mark laughed when I said this. "Anne has no sympathy for the Queen," he said. "She is refusing to be the King's mistress for just one reason. She wants to be his wife, and she will settle for nothing less."

That is nonsense, of course. Henry is married to Queen Catherine, and the Church does not allow marriage vows to be broken. They will be man and wife for ever.

23rd August 1526

Mama says I am a woman now. I was frightened when I found traces of blood and ran to her because I thought I was ill, but she told me it's a very important part of growing up. I felt angry at first. Couldn't I have had a choice about whether I wanted to grow up? I have always wanted to have the same freedom as my brothers, to run about and ride and shoot, but Mama shook her head today, and said women have more important things to do. Perhaps it will not be too bad. The ladies of the court ride horses and fly hawks and go hunting, I suppose. In any case, I cannot change my life, any more than I can stop the winds blowing or the sun shining, so I will enjoy whatever there is to enjoy.

Rosanna has fallen in love with Diego Luiz de Frontera, the son of one of the Spanish attendants who came over from Granada with the Queen. She blushes and says it is not serious, but she cannot keep her eyes off him. He is very handsome, slim and broad-shouldered, with dark hair and eyes. I can see she is very happy.

Poor Princess Mary will not be happy. The French king, Francis I, wants to marry again because his wife died two years ago, and he has offered his hand as a husband for Mary. King Henry is delighted and so is Cardinal Wolsey.

The Queen, however, is not delighted at all. The French have always been enemies of Spain, so she does not want her daughter to marry their king. Besides, Mary is still only ten, and Francis is even older than the Emperor Charles. He could be her grandfather.

20th February 1527

Today is my thirteenth birthday – and I have been appointed a Lady of Court, to wait on the Queen! In a way it is nothing new, as I have always helped Rosanna and Mama, but I feel very grown-up, with my hair braided neatly under an embroidered cap, a present from Rosanna. Mama gave me a new gown, much more elaborate than any of my childhood dresses, and although I have always preferred boyish things, I must admit, this lovely dress is a pleasure. I specially like the slashed and embroidered over-sleeves that show the brocaded fabric underneath. They can be changed if they become soiled, as they are easier to clean than an entire gown. Mama gave me three pairs of sleeves, but my favourites are the pale-green silk ones, embroidered in blue and silver-white.

How strange it is to feel like a court lady! Suddenly I am included in the gossip instead of being sent away like a little girl, and I am starting to understand how things are done. People who want a favour of the King used to ask Queen Catherine to put in a word for them, but now they ask Anne Boleyn instead, knowing she is the one Henry listens to.

The Queen ignores all this. Since Christmas I have been going out with her and some other ladies almost every day, helping her to distribute charity among the crowds who flock to see her. Whatever her private worries may be, she is always serene and kind, and the common people adore her. They have probably heard the rumours about Anne, for gossip can never be stopped, but it has merely made them more protective of their true queen.

10th April 1527

We have been at Hampton Court all through the winter. I love this place. The frosty daylight shines in through all its great windows, and it is a joy to walk through its grounds and see the spring flowers blooming.

A delegation is here from France to talk about Mary's marriage to the French king. Their ambassador said an extraordinary thing. He asked whether Mary really is the King's legitimate daughter. The courtiers who were listening dared not even glance at each other, they were so embarrassed. How can anyone doubt that Mary is the child of Henry and Catherine of Aragon?

Rosanna explained later what the ambassador meant. Apparently the King is trying to claim that he was never legally married to Catherine. He has found a passage in the Bible that says it is unlawful for a man to marry his brother's wife – and Catherine was of course married to Henry's elder brother, Arthur, for a few months. Arthur then died, and Catherine waited for years before it was decided that she could marry Henry, who had always been her true love.

Everything has changed now. Henry is trying to wriggle out of his marriage so he can take Anne as his new wife. And the only way he can do this is to declare his marriage to Queen Catherine illegal. I have never seen Mama so furious. "What a way to treat her!" she fumed. "And after all she has done for him! She ran the country while he was away at his silly war with France, she beat the Scots, she has advised him wisely for all these years, she has brought him the love of the people – and he will throw all this away for some obstinate girl who will not give in to him? The man is insane!"

17th April 1527

Cardinal Wolsey has assured the French that Mary is indeed the King's rightful daughter. I am glad. But I still do not want her to marry that old man.

Meanwhile, there is scandalous news. King Henry has asked Anne Boleyn to be his wife! How *can* he? Obviously he thinks he can dissolve his marriage to Catherine, but that is hardly the point. His determination to marry Anne astounds everyone. He has had mistresses before, many of them – we are all used to that – but to take this girl as a *wife* seems extraordinary. She is no more than a court servant, like the rest of us. Her family has distant royal connections, but whose has not? My own family cannot be called aristocratic – after all, we are not even English. But Mama is from a titled Spanish family, and her uncle was for many years the Spanish ambassador. Anne's father married Elizabeth Howard, of an old titled family, but he himself came of tradesmen. The whole court is buzzing with speculation about what will happen next.

2nd May 1527

The betrothal between Mary and the French king has been agreed. There was a banquet last night, and the dancing and drinking went on long afterwards. When the King was dancing with his daughter, he suddenly pulled off Mary's jewelled cap and let the wavy length of her fair hair fall free, as if to show off her beauty. Everyone laughed and applauded. Poor Mary, though. I would not be in her place, bound to marry an old man whom she has never met.

17th May 1527

King Henry and Cardinal Wolsey are meeting at Westminster with William Warham, the Archbishop of Canterbury, to talk about the King's marriage. Henry wants Cardinal Wolsey to put the question to the Pope for his decision, but the Cardinal was horrified at the whole idea. He cannot refuse the King's request, though. Nobody can refuse the King anything – except the Pope, of course.

Tonight I asked Mama what it says in the Bible about a man who marries his brother's wife. She took down our own Bible and turned to Leviticus, and ran her finger down the pages. We stared at the close-printed lines by the candle's light. Most of the chapters were about sacrifice and burnt offerings, but then she came to the rules by which a man must live if he is to be pure. "This is it," she said. We read the words of chapter 20, verse 21 together:

Qui duxerit uxorem fratris sui, rem facit illicitam, turpitudinem fratris sui revelavit absque liberis sunt.

And if a man shall take his brother's wife, it is an unclean thing; he hath uncovered his brother's nakedness; they shall be childless.

"You see?" Mama said. "Henry thinks he has sinned in marrying Catherine, who was his brother's wife. And he fears that God's punishment for that is to deny him a son."

I found the whole chapter very frightening. It showed a fierce and unforgiving God, greedy for blood and the smoke of burnt meat. Then I was scared again, this time by my own dislike of it. After all, the Bible is holy. We do not have the choice to believe or not believe. As a mere human being, I dare not imagine how the Lord God will judge our king, who only started to fear that he had sinned when his desires were moving elsewhere.

2nd June 1527

The Pope is in prison! Emperor Charles has been campaigning in Italy, and last month his soldiers went on a mutinous rampage and sacked the city of Rome. The men were unpaid and starving, we hear, but all the same it seems a terrible thing to do. The Holy Father is locked up in a fortress called Castel San Angelo, and the Emperor has done nothing to free him, merely apologized. We all think he has lost control of his army.

Papa laughed when he heard. "So the King is out of luck!" he said. While Pope Clement remains imprisoned, he cannot judge on the question of Henry Tudor's marriage. And Henry cannot marry Anne until the Pope agrees that his previous marriage is ended.

The King is furious, of course. If the Pope cannot give a judgement on his case, then somebody must. He is sending Wolsey to France to set up a ruling council with the other cardinals in Avignon. Can they really act without Pope Clement's authority? Most people think it is impossible, but preparations have started for Wolsey's departure. George Cavendish will be with the party, and he is rushing about like a man demented, organizing horses and mules, baggage and equipment.

Mama is equally busy with the provision of black velvet coats for the clerical gentlemen who will go with the Cardinal, and we are all stitching frantically, even I who am no kind of needlewoman compared with Mama. At least I can sew a straight seam nowadays. Anne Boleyn herself sews with us, and her fingers are very quick and neat. Until this business is decided, she remains one of the Queen's ladies, of no more importance than the rest of us. But of course everyone watches her, and malicious gossip abounds.

6th June 1527

Henry has sent Anne away to her parents' home in Hever. I suppose he feels it is time to remove her from being no more than a serving lady.

22nd June 1527

King Henry went to see Catherine today, and asked her to release him and retire from being queen.

Heavens, what a rumpus! The Queen wept like a thing demented, and screamed at him that she was and always would be his legal wife. Henry emerged from her chambers looking ruffled and angry. I do not feel much sympathy for him. From what Mama has told me, Catherine went through years of hardship and neglect before he married her, and she would rather die than let him cast her off. She is sending a messenger to ask her nephew, the Emperor Charles, if he will help her. Since Charles is responsible for imprisoning the Pope, he can presumably talk to him and perhaps persuade him not to dissolve her marriage. The messenger is one of Catherine's most trusted servants, a man named Felipez.

24th June 1527

Henry found out about the messenger. I expect one of Anne Boleyn's supporters told him. He sent riders galloping after the man all the way to Dover, but when they got there Felipez was already aboard a ship that had sailed. So the Emperor will get to hear of his aunt's plight. I cannot imagine that he will do much about it, though. He is too busy fighting wars.

16th July 1527

The question of Henry's marriage has come to the notice of the English Parliament as well as to the Church. Thomas More, the Lord Chancellor, has told the King his marriage cannot be called illegal. John Fisher, the Bishop of Rochester, has said the same thing. Henry is not pleased.

15th September 1527

The French ambassadors are here for more negotiations about Mary's marriage. It was a state occasion, so Henry and Catherine sat side by side to watch a masque performed by children, smiling as though nothing could be wrong between them. They still look a handsome couple, though both of them are bulkier in the body than they once were. I think they are still fond of each other, for Henry visits his wife in her chambers quite often. Perhaps this business about Anne will blow over. I hope so.

16th December 1527

The Pope has been freed. Nobody knows whether the Emperor spoke to him on Catherine's behalf, and meanwhile King Henry has sent his secretary, William Knight, to Rome. They say he bears a message asking His Holiness to declare that Henry may marry any other woman, providing his marriage to Catherine is annulled.

Cardinal Wolsey is back from his meeting with the Cardinals in Avignon, having achieved nothing. As the King's closest adviser, he does not expect Henry to send messages to the Pope without consulting him, and he looks very displeased.

1st January 1528

On this New Year's morning, Rosanna was married to her true love, Diego Luiz de Frontera, in the chapel here at Greenwich. Mama wept tears of happiness, and then she turned to me and said, "God willing, you will be next, Ellie."

I am nearly fourteen, well old enough to be married, but I still find it hard to take the idea seriously. There are constant flirtations among the courtiers, and I suppose it would be easy enough to show an interest in one of them, but they are so much the same as each other – well-dressed, amusing, expert in all the graces of court life, and delighting in malicious gossip. I can see why Mama married my father, a Frenchman who lived by his own skills and had no real respect for any of them. And why should I hurry? I enjoy my music, and play often for the Queen now – even for the King sometimes, though his changing moods can be alarming.

As for Rosanna – she looked lovely, in a gown of white silk sewn with small pearls, and her dark hair loose. With Diego beside her, handsome in an embroidered doublet of black velvet, she seemed utterly blissful. They will have their own room now, but they go on serving the Queen in the same way. Does marriage really make such a difference? Yes, perhaps it does – but I still find it hard to imagine.

24th February 1528

The Pope has agreed to let Wolsey and one other cardinal hear the King's case against Queen Catherine in England. The other cardinal will be Lorenzo Campeggio, who has to come from Rome. They say the poor man suffers dreadfully from gout, so his journey is likely to be a slow and painful one. The case will not be heard for a while, so perhaps the weather will be kinder by the time he sets out.

At Henry's command, Wolsey has made a public announcement about "the King's great matter", as it is being called. The common people in the cities and the countryside now know that their king is seeking to escape from his marriage to Catherine. But their loyalty is to the Queen. I was with her this afternoon when she rode out, and all along the way crowds gathered to wish her success over her enemies. Henry is scowling and angry. Mama says he fears that Catherine will stir up a rebellion against him. In the early days of their marriage he often turned to her for advice on what he should do, and he knows she is clear-minded and politically astute. She would do nothing to harm him, though. He is her husband and her lord, and she loves him.

4th June 1528

The sweating sickness has come to London. It is a bad outbreak, and everyone is thrown into a panic. The King is very afraid of this disease. I suppose because it killed his brother, Arthur. He has ordered that we must be ready to leave at any moment.

14th June 1528

One of the court ladies has fallen ill with the sickness, so we will leave tomorrow. Anne is still with her parents at Hever, so she at least will be safe. I do not know where the rest of us will go, but we are frantically packing.

15th June 1528

Papa is ill. When we got up early this morning, he was shivering, although his skin was burning hot. He tried to tell us it was nothing serious, but his teeth chattered as he spoke, and it was obvious that he could not manage two days of riding. Mama will stay with him, but I have been ordered to go with the royal party. Diego and Rosanna will be with us as well. I am scribbling this quickly, as we are almost ready to leave. My poor parents – I am frantic with worry about both of them.

17th June 1528

We are in a place called Tittenhanger, in Hertfordshire, at the house of the Abbot of St Albans. The King thinks we will be safe from the sickness here. My mind is constantly with Mama and Papa, left behind to cope as best they can. A lot of the servants are still there, so at least somebody will fetch water and food for them, but I am full of fear.

23rd June 1528

A rider arrived in the middle of last night to tell the King that Anne Boleyn has the sickness, but then he added the terrible, casual words, "And I regret to say Michel Valjean has expired. Your good jester, sire."

I burst into tears. The other ladies took me out of the room and tried to comfort me. One of them ran for Rosanna and told her, and we wept together. She has Diego, though, so she is not alone with her grief. It is late now, and the candle is almost burned out, but I cannot stop weeping. Papa seems so real in my mind, with his thin, lively face, but I will never see him again, never watch his quick fingers over the lute strings, never laugh at his wit, never marvel at a new story. The messenger said my mother was somewhat ill with the same sickness but is now recovering. I thank the good Lord for that – to lose her as well would be too much to bear.

Rosanna did what she could to comfort me. Papa has been spared the pains of old age, she pointed out. He will not suffer stiffness of the joints and toothache and the slow loss of his sight as most people do. This is true, and I suppose I am merely selfish in my constant weeping. The loss of my dear father is like an injury to my spirit, and the soreness of it goes on and on.

28th June 1528

We hear that Anne Boleyn's attack was only a slight one, though her sister's husband, William Carey, died of the sickness. Anne had the best of attention. Henry's own doctor was out tending the sick, but he sent Dr Butts to her at once. This morning he despatched a rider with a haunch of venison to assist her recovery.

We are packing to go back to London, but it will be a sad return.

2nd August 1528

We arrived back yesterday. Mama and I wept together. The room she shared with Papa seems so empty now. I wish I could have said a better goodbye to him than the few rushed words before we had to leave.

Anne Boleyn is no longer in the Queen's service. King Henry has given her an apartment of her own, a small place off the tiltyard in Greenwich Palace, where he may see her whenever he chooses. Mama, in the midst of her own grief, is outraged at this new insult to the Queen.

9th October 1528

Cardinal Campeggio arrived today, after two months of travelling. I thought there would be a big reception for him, as he is to assist Wolsey in deciding on the question of the King's marriage, but this was not the case. He came into London by way of the river, on a barge that had no special decoration, and took to his bed at once. Such a long journey must have been agony for a man who suffers from gout.

It is more than three months since Papa died, but I still miss him. I feel that I shall never be light-hearted again.

13th October 1528

Queen Catherine spoke to me kindly today. "Your father would not want to see you so sad, Elinor," she said. My eyes filled with tears again, but she told me something I had never thought of. "Every woman carries grief," she said. "It is like a fire, painful at first. But when you become used to it, you will find it a source of strength." I thought of how much grief she has known in her life, and made her a deep curtsey. "God go with you," she said, and blessed me.

24th October 1528

Wolsey and Campeggio came to see Catherine today. I know now that they wanted her to enter a nunnery so that Henry would be free to marry Anne, and she refused, but at the time I only heard the raised voices and the anger. The two men came out looking red-faced and annoyed, and went off to report their failure to the King.

I would not be in their shoes. Henry's temper has been more than usually short lately, as he is troubled by an injury to his leg, the result of a fall from his horse in the summer. The wound is ulcerated and will not heal, and he hates to be less than perfectly fit and healthy.

29th October 1528

A letter was brought to the Queen this afternoon. She said nothing when she read it, but she looked very distressed. Mama told me afterwards that it came from the Privy Council. They have advised the King to separate himself from Catherine completely. They have also told him he should remove Princess Mary from her company.

12th November 1528

King Henry did a strange thing today. He threw open Bridewell Palace and invited the common people to come in. And in they came, of course, with their smelly clothes and dirty faces, their baskets and bundles and babies and dogs, staring about them at the rich hangings and the gilded ceiling. The King entered and stood before the throne, wearing his robes of state. He told them of his need to have a son who would rule England after him, then he spoke warmly of Catherine. Were he to have his time over again, he said, he would marry no other – but he had to think of the future. He explained his case for taking a new wife, and the people stared at him in a mixture of respect and astonishment. Some of them nodded as he spoke, and at the end there were shouts of "God Save the King!" But there were sideways glances among them as they were ushered down the steps and back into the street.

Not even Henry himself can make them like Anne Boleyn. She is too close to their own common blood to command their respect. Going out among the last of them, I heard one woman murmur to another, "She is nothing but a scheming harlot." And there are many at court who would agree.

15th November 1528

This is a dreadful day. The King has commanded that I must leave the Queen's service and join Anne Boleyn's household. He is moving her from Greenwich to a much grander house in the Strand, with a garden that runs down to the river. She has demanded that most of the younger ladies shall wait upon her, and I am among them. Rosanna was not chosen, so I will not even have the company of my sister.

I am full of resentment. It is a bitter thing to have to serve a fellow servant, no matter how she has risen in the world. I will have to leave Mama, too, for she, like Rosanna and Diego, will stay with the Queen.

The poor Queen – her chambers will seem empty and dull without so many of the lively girls who have been like a family to her. She is 43 now, the same age as Mama. Maria de Salinas is still with her, but she is far older. A staff of new ladies will be chosen by Wolsey and the King, and I know what that means. Their function will be to spy on the Queen and report back to their masters on whatever she says and does. I am glad Rosanna and Mama will be with her, even though I shall miss them.

I almost regret the years spent learning my music and dancing, and the gaiety of heart that led me to laugh and make up stories. Look where it has led me! But I seem to hear Papa assuring me that music lasts longer than people do. He is right, of course. I will take up my lute and play for my own comfort, for there is no other.

Christmas 1528

After a few weeks at the Strand house, we have come here to Greenwich Palace for the Christmas period. My lady Anne is housed in separate quarters from the rest of the court, and we are perpetually busy, providing refreshments and entertaining her constant stream of visitors. The Queen is in a different part of the palace (with Mama and Rosanna, thank goodness) and she appears with the King when guests are invited, to give the impression that things are continuing as normal. I do not see much of these occasions, for I have to play and sing as commanded by Her Ladyship. My spirit of goodwill is sadly lacking.

8th January 1529

Christmas is over, and I am back at the house in the Strand. When I picked up one of Mistress Anne's discarded dresses this morning I found under it a book by Simon Fish, called *The Supplication of Beggars*. I looked into its pages, and saw that it was in favour of the Bible being translated into English so that any common person may read it. They say Mr Fish had to leave the country, and I am not surprised. To write such a thing is rank heresy. I made the sign of the cross and returned the book to its place. Latin has always been the language of religion. What will happen to the authority of the Church if people start to take the mysteries of God into their own hands? The Pope will surely never allow it.

The people of England are forbidden to read heretical books, yet the King does not mind Anne flaunting them under his nose. Even worse, he reads them himself. There is one called *The Obedience of a Christian Man, and How Kings Ought to Govern*, by William Tynedale. I picked it up from beside Henry's chair the other day, knowing nothing of its contents. Then I found that Mr Tyndale has actually translated the Bible into English! What's more, he says a ruling monarch should have authority over the Church in his country – he need not bow to the authority of the Pope. No wonder King Henry finds it interesting. If he could make himself head of the English Church, he would not have to ask permission from Rome to divorce his wife.

18th February 1529

Nobody will take the responsibility of deciding on the King's case against Catherine. Campeggio now says he is not empowered to make any judgement without referring to the Pope – and the Pope is ill, we hear, and unable to attend to any questions at all. Henry banged his fist on the table when he heard about this. He is furiously impatient, and although my sympathies are for the Queen, I can see how he feels. These endless delays are unbearable.

20th February 1529

Today is my fifteenth birthday. I have not told anyone here, for I have no particular friends. I wish so much that I could have stayed in Greenwich, with all my family together as we were at Christmas.

When the daily rider came from there this morning with messages for Anne, he gave me letters from Mama and Rosanna, and some exciting packages. Daniel sent me a bird he had carved from a piece of wood, and little William had wrapped up a pomegranate. From Mama I had a pair of gloves, intricately worked with her beautiful embroidery, and Rosanna – dear Rosanna! – sent me a diary. She put a letter in with it, saying she thought I might like to write things down, now I am on my own in this place. "A diary is not as good as a friend," she said, "but it can help if there are times when you are lonely."

She is quite right, of course. I wonder if she knows I have been keeping a diary all this time. My disused Latin book bulges now with the bits of paper I have tucked into it. I think I will copy them all into my new, proper diary. It will be something to do in the dark evenings, and my writing is neater now than it was when I was eleven. Mama's letter said the Queen sends her good wishes for my birthday. I was very thrilled by that.

She went on to say the Queen knows of a document written by the old Pope Julius II, who was alive many years ago when Catherine was married to Henry's brother, Arthur. Arthur died only six months after their marriage, and the Pope's document was written to give Catherine permission to marry Henry. This means Henry cannot possibly say his marriage to Catherine was illegal. It proves absolutely that the Queen is his true wife, and has every right to remain so.

There are difficulties, though. The document is now in Spain. It was among the papers of my great-uncle, Rodrigo De Puebla, and when he died everything was returned to his home country to be looked after by the Emperor Charles. The Queen needs to have it in her own hands, of course, but Henry will not want her to possess such a powerful piece of evidence. If the Emperor sends the document to England, Catherine fears it will be conveniently lost. Mama says she is hoping her nephew, the Emperor, will think of something.

27th March 1529

Although Anne likes to hear me play and sing, she does not confide in me at all. I can hardly blame her – she must know I still love Queen Catherine. But her other ladies gossip, even though they have been picked for their loyalty to Anne, so I hear a lot about the Queen's "obstructive attitude", as they call it, and the irritating inactivity of the Pope.

The Holy Father is said to be recovering from his illness, but he is perhaps not fully in charge of things yet for he has agreed that Wolsey and Campeggio may call a court at Westminster for a hearing of "the King's great matter". They have been given the power to judge on the Pope's behalf. Anne and her friends are delighted, naturally. They are sure the case will go against Catherine, and Henry will then be free to marry Anne. I do not share their certainty. The Queen is a shrewd and determined fighter, and the people of England are on her side.

All the same, things are difficult for her. Mama's last letter says the Emperor listened to her request about the old Pope's document. Understanding that the original might be intercepted and destroyed, he sent a *copy* of it to London, but ensured that it was signed by the most eminent bishops in Spain, testifying that it was a genuine reproduction of the original. Surely that should have been good enough? But when Henry and Wolsey saw it, they at once dismissed it as a forgery.

20th May 1529

The cardinals' court really is going to take place in Westminster. We have to move my lady Anne's household to Hever for the duration of the hearing, as the King feels she should be away from London. I have little time to write – there is so much to be packed and organized. Anne is agitated and upset, saying she wants to stay here. She seems deeply nervous about the hearing. She knows how warmly the people regard their queen, and knows too that if the case goes in Catherine's favour that will be the end of her own hopes.

The Queen has chosen the lawyers who will defend her. They are the bishops of Ely and St Asaph, old Archbishop Warham of Canterbury, and her faithful friend John Fisher, Bishop of Rochester. They sound impressive – but the King may have even more important men on his side.

18th June 1529

Hever Castle is a lovely place. It looks forbidding from outside, with its sheer walls rising from a moat that runs all round it, but there are also beautiful gardens all around, and meadows that run down to the little river. They are full of buttercups and cow parsley, and there is no sound except for the birds singing. It is so good to be away from the noisy centre of London, with its clatter of hooves and constant rattle of wheels over cobblestones. The summer evenings are warm, and the scent of fresh-scythed hay is sweet. I am happy here.

So happy. I have met someone I love. His name is Tom Freeman. He was out with a couple of dogs early one morning when I was walking by the willow trees along the river. He smiled when he saw me and said, "Dabbling in the dew?"

I sang him a snatch of the old song as a reply: "Makes the milkmaids fair." And he joined in. He has a lovely voice, deep but very sweet, like dark honey.

We both laughed when the song came to an end. He has brown hair that curls like the coats of his retrievers, and his eyes are grey. He smiled and said he didn't usually burst into song with strangers. I said I didn't, either. I was wearing an old dress, and the hem was all wet with the dew on the long grass. I hadn't even braided my hair, and it was hanging loose down my back, but he didn't seem to mind. "Midsummer madness," he said. "The sun hardly above the trees, and here we stand, singing like a pair of cuckoos."

I said, "Cuckoos don't sing, they just cuckoo," and he said it probably sounded like song to them.

I wish we were a pair of cuckoos. I'd like to fly away with him, and leave this court and all its scheming people behind. He is the blacksmith here at Hever. Mostly he shoes the horses and doctors them for any injury or illness, but he makes things as well – cart-springs, gate hinges, tools for the farm workers. I went with him into the smithy where he works. It was very cool in there, as the forge fire was not lit. He kissed me. I never thought I would want a stranger to do that, but Tom does not seem like a stranger. I feel as if I have known him for ever.

I keep thinking about our meeting. I remember every word of what he said and what I said, and reliving it has warmed me all day. One of Anne's ladies looked at me and asked, "Why are you smiling?" I said

I didn't know. My cuckoo morning is not for sharing with people who gossip so maliciously about each other, and would do about me as well, given half a chance.

21st July 1529

The King's case is being heard at Westminster. Riders come daily with messages for Madam Anne. Most of them are in Henry's bold hand, but today there was also a letter for me from Mama. Queen Catherine, she says, appeared just once before the court. She fell on her knees and made a passionate speech, declaring her love for Henry and her belief in the truth of her marriage. After that she left the court on the arm of one of her gentlemen, and has refused to return. They hope a judgement will be made in two days' time. I do hope so. And I hope they decide in favour of the Queen.

23rd July 1529

The trial has come to an end, but nothing has been decided. Campeggio shocked everyone by announcing that the Pope had changed his mind about allowing any cardinal to give judgement. The ruling would have to be considered in Rome. And the papal court in Rome always enjoyed a summer break of three months, so nothing further could be done until October. The King was so enraged that he stormed out of the court.

When Anne Boleyn read the letter that came from Henry this evening, her pale face flushed with fury. She said some extremely rude things about Campeggio. "And as to Wolsey, he is nothing more than a broken reed," she added. "Useless."

She has always hated Wolsey, but since receiving the letter, she has been pacing about in such a tempest of anger that none of us dares speak to her.

25th July 1529

Tom and I have met in the early morning for the last two days. I would like to see him more often, but the household is in a turmoil of packing and preparation, and I am frantically busy. The hearing at Westminster delayed our departure for the summer progress, and Anne is all impatience to set off. She is looking forward to it with special excitement, as Queen Catherine will be left behind this year. Henry has chosen to travel with Anne, parading her before the people as his chosen consort and maybe his future queen, so she is of course delighted.

Tom will be with us, thank goodness. King Henry has noticed that he cares for the horses well, and there is no time to send for his own blacksmith, who did not come with Anne's party to Hever. I am so glad!

14th August 1529

There is hardly time to write a word. We are constantly moving from one great house to another. Waltham Abbey, Barnet, Holborn, Windsor, Reading, Woodstock – there seems no end to the packing and unpacking. We will return to Greenwich in October, but meanwhile we are royal travellers, welcomed by our hosts wherever we go.

The common people are less enthusiastic. Anne, usually carried in a litter with the curtains drawn back so she can be seen, waves and smiles to them, but they do not smile back. Many of them scowl as our procession passes through their villages, and some shout abusive words, then duck away quickly before they can be seen and arrested. Their opinion is very clear. To them, Catherine is the only rightful queen.

20th September 1529

We are at Grafton in Northamptonshire, housed in a royal hunting lodge in the woods. Cardinal Campeggio came on a farewell visit to the King, as he has been recalled to Rome now that the fruitless trial is over. Wolsey arrived as well, but we were not instructed to prepare any accommodation for him. Campeggio was escorted to his quarters, but Wolsey was left standing in the courtyard on his own. Some of the ladies were secretly giggling, but I felt terribly sorry for the poor man. Fortunately, Sir Henry Norris came out and offered the Cardinal his own room.

This discourtesy is my lady Anne's doing, of course. Her loathing of Wolsey gets more and more intense. As if to make up for her rudeness, Henry asked Wolsey to meet with him and the Boleyn supporters later in the afternoon. I glimpsed the Cardinal going in through the door to the room where the Dukes of Suffolk, Norfolk and Rochester were assembled with others, and saw how he fell on his knees before the King. Henry put both his hands under Wolsey's elbows, helping him to rise. Then the door closed, cutting off my view.

I must go and help set the tables with gold plate and wine goblets. There is to be a great dinner tonight for Campeggio's departure. Henry has no cause to like him, but he will not neglect the proper courtesies.

21st September 1529

Anne Boleyn was sulky and out of humour all through the banquet yesterday evening, darting venomous glances at Wolsey and making slighting remarks. At one point Henry said to her in mock surprise, "I perceive you are not the Cardinal's friend." Anne retorted that she could not be Wolsey's friend, because he treated the King so badly. That is complete nonsense, of course. Wolsey would do anything for the King, and we all know it.

This morning she persuaded Henry to go hunting, just at the time when Wolsey and Campeggio had to depart. The King leaned down from his horse to bid them farewell, and spoke in warm terms, but it was a scant and inadequate way to take his leave of two eminent men.

4th October 1529

We are at Greenwich Palace, all of us together. It is so good to be with Mama and Rosanna and the boys again, for Queen Catherine is here, even though Henry spends most of his time with Anne. And Tom is to stay with us! He cured Anne's favourite horse when it went lame on progress, so she has demanded that he must be her personal blacksmith from now on. I thought her father might be annoyed, for he will not easily find another man with Tom's skills, but he made no objection. I suppose he has little choice but to fall in with his daughter's whims. If she marries the King, she will make her whole family rich and famous.

Henry is not troubled about such small matters as a new blacksmith, for he has a new cause for fury. His letters to Anne disappeared at the time when Campeggio left, and he is sure they were stolen.

I heard him bellowing last night that the whole court is corrupt and he can trust nobody. But then, he had drunk a great amount of wine.

His mood improved this morning, after two men had been to see him. They spoke of Thomas Cranmer, a friend of theirs who has new ideas on the judgement of the King's case. This Cranmer contends that it does not have to be heard by the Pope or even by an assembly of cardinals. The clerics of England's own universities, he says, have the power to decide, and if the Archbishop of Canterbury should pronounce King Henry's marriage invalid, then invalid it is. When I heard this, my mind flew back to William Tynedale's book and the idea that the King can be head of the English Church. Perhaps Henry is thinking of it as well. He has commanded Cranmer to come and see him, and he seems much excited.

7th October 1529

The King has been in constant talks with Thomas Cranmer, who is now lodged at the house of Anne's father, Lord Rochford. Evidently his new friend has given him new ideas, for we hear that Henry intends to charge Cardinal Wolsey with something called praemunire. I asked one of the court gentlemen what it means, and he said it is the crime of asking a foreign power to judge on something that should be a nation's own business. I suppose this refers to the Pope's judgement on Henry's divorce. Rome is not England.

Cranmer, like Tynedale, seems to think the King can be his own judge, backed by the clerics of the English universities. It still sounds like heresy to me.

9th October 1529

King Henry has indeed charged Wolsey with praemunire. He has stripped him of his office as Lord Chancellor of England, and we are all stunned. The Cardinal himself is terribly upset. He has given almost all of his property to the King in an effort to placate him, including his great house called York Place, but the King remains adamant. Wolsey will retire to his one remaining home, a modest house in Esher, in Surrey.

Anne is delighted at his fall. I don't know why she hates Wolsey so much, but Rosanna tells me it is because of something that happened years ago, when Anne was in love with young Henry Percy. Even then, the King wanted her for himself, but he did not choose to say so. He left it to Wolsey to tell Anne she was not a suitable bride for a young man from a noble family and to pack her off to her parents at Hever. I think Wolsey did Anne a favour, for had she married Percy, she would have settled down with him and never dreamed of being the Queen of England – but she seems unconcerned about that. Wolsey slighted her, and she has never forgiven him. And at last she has had her revenge.

17th October 1529

A new Spanish ambassador has arrived. He is called Eustache Chapuys. He spent all morning in conference with Queen Catherine. Anne hates him. She knows an enemy when she sees one, and Chapuys has a hard, confident look about him. He is not impressed by Anne's influence with the King, and he does not mind what he says, either. Already he has been heard to refer to Anne Boleyn as "the concubine", which is a rather insulting way of referring to a man's mistress.

2nd November 1529

The King is delighted with Wolsey's house, York Place. He took Anne to see it on the very day it came into his hands. He is going to turn it into a palace for her, renaming it as Whitehall. Anne is ecstatic – but despite that, she still wants to see the Cardinal in prison or even executed. She nags Henry about it constantly, but without much success. The gift of the palace has calmed the King's temper, and he seems disinclined to punish Wolsey any further. He will allow him to keep his office as Archbishop of York, and Anne will have to be satisfied with her new house.

The place is already full of workmen making the necessary alterations. Anne wants to move in at once, not waiting for them to finish. She cannot wait to have her own court. Once installed in Whitehall, she will be queen in everything except name.

10th December 1529

What an upheaval it has been! We have all been working day and night to get everything exactly as my lady wants it.

Most of the time, she seems pleased with the way things are going, and so she should be, but there are occasional explosions of temper. She was enraged yesterday when she found out that Catherine still mends Henry's shirts. Anne herself is a good needlewoman, and she screamed protests at him.

Henry roared back at her on this occasion, but he does not seem seriously bothered by these outbursts. He continues to shower presents on her, and two days ago he honoured Anne's father with the title of Earl of Wiltshire. Her brother George becomes Viscount Rochford and Anne herself is to be known as the Lady Anne Boleyn – but she is not satisfied. She is impatient to become England's true queen, and she is careless of who listens as she argues with Henry. I heard her this very evening, shouting at him that she might by now be married to some other man, by whom she could have had children.

This was cruel of her. She knows how raw the King's feelings are on that subject – and after all, he is moving heaven and earth to try to make her his queen. It perplexes me that he thinks she is worth all this massive upheaval and trouble, but I suppose he loves her.

30th December 1529

News reaches us that Cardinal Wolsey is gravely ill. King Henry was saddened to hear it, for he and Wolsey are old friends, despite the differences that now part them. He said he would not lose him for £20,000. He gave orders for his own physician, Dr Butts, to attend the sick man, and in front of all of us he turned to Anne and told her she must send the Cardinal a token of her esteem. She did not argue, but meekly detached a tablet of gold from her belt and handed it to the King.

I thought she would resent being made to give such a valuable gift to Wolsey, but at dinner in the great hall tonight one of her ladies mentioned the episode, and Anne laughed. That was nothing, she said. It would cost her more than £20,000 in bribes before she had done with Wolsey. I saw Chapuys raise his head sharply and stare at her. He, as the Spanish ambassador, is of course on Catherine's side in all this. He will doubtless tell the Queen that Anne intends to bribe people so as to make sure Wolsey's downfall is complete, and Catherine will tell the Emperor Charles in the hope that he will make Henry see what a scheming minx Anne is. But Anne knows all that, and she does not care. She is certain now that she will soon hold all the power.

Oh why did the Pope not make a decision when this first started? The Holy Father's dithering has let the whole thing grow into a monstrous enmity between himself and King Henry. In order to get his own way, the King seems ready to flout the whole authority of the Catholic Church, and that must surely be the ultimate sin. Where will it all end?

4th March 1530

I did not want to come to Anne's household at Whitehall, for it meant another parting with my family, but Tom is here as well. He and I have seen each other every day, so these have been happy months. This place is not like Hever, though. There are no gardens, no meadows, no clear little river, only the grey width of the Thames, with all its boats and barges.

Rosanna is expecting a baby in the autumn. I shall be an aunt! Strangely, I found that I envied her. I never thought I would want marriage and children, being a restless girl who always wanted to be a boy – but in a way, I have had my wish. Anne regards me as her jester and entertainer, a singer and player who can dispel bad moods and bring amusement – but I had not imagined being in the service of a peevish, moody woman who wants nothing but to become Henry's queen. I grew up in the tempestuous warmth of Henry's court, with its masques and dances, its summer storms of fury and its gales of laughter, but this household is a tight-lipped one in which people have learned to be careful what they say.

Perhaps I am not by nature a court lady. Papa came from a family of troubadours, travelling from one country to another, with no expectation of becoming rich or powerful. When Mama first knew about Tom, she felt she had to remind me that a blacksmith would not bring me the advantages that would come through marrying an aristocratic husband – but she smiled as she said it, and I knew she was not very serious.

Tom and I share a dream that one day we will leave the King's service, if he will release us, and live in some small place of our own. Perhaps it will never be more than a dream, but we love thinking about it, planning what crops we will grow and where we will keep the pig and the cow, and whether we can afford a horse.

The dream may never come true, but at least it makes us happy. The King, on the other hand, looks increasingly irritable. During these winter months there have been some violent quarrels between him and Anne. She has always been sharp-tongued, and he admired her for that at first, liking her spirit, but there have been times when I have held my breath at some cheeky response of hers. After all, Henry is the king, and he commands respect, even from those he loves.

He repented of his severity to Wolsey, who has been ill throughout the winter, for at heart he has a great regard for his old friend and adviser. He sent him a formal pardon last week, though the Cardinal is still banned from any return to court. Anne was furious, naturally, and made some dark remarks to the effect that she had not finished with Wolsey yet. I think uneasily of her reference to the costs of bribery, and wonder what she is planning. Meanwhile, the Cardinal's health is improving a little. Perhaps the small sign of Henry's forgiveness has put new heart into him.

28th March 1530

Today has given me a personal cause to dislike the Boleyn family. Anne's brother George caught me by the waist and pulled me to him, causing me to spill wine down my skirt from the jug I was carrying. He turned my head with his strong hand and pressed a kiss on my mouth, asking why I chose to be so chaste and superior. I told him I was betrothed – though that is not strictly true – and tried to free myself from his grasp. He demanded to know who my chosen sweetheart was, but I would not tell him, for fear he would get Tom sent away. He released me at last, but not until I had endured much of his kissing and pawing of my body. I am a strong girl and had he been any ordinary man I would have used my fists and feet to send him packing, but he is Lord Rochford, much favoured by the King, and I dared not give him cause for complaint. Tom is furious.

20th July 1530

We hear that all the lords of England, Wolsey included, signed a petition to the Pope some weeks ago, asking him to decide in favour of dissolving the King's marriage. I was surprised to hear this of Wolsey, who has never liked Anne Boleyn, but I suppose he is anxious to keep in King Henry's favour. But it was no good, for his Holiness still refuses to consider a divorce. The Emperor naturally wants him to come down on the side of the Queen, and I suppose the Holy Father is in a quandary, not wishing to offend either of these powerful men. Henry has threatened to marry Anne whether he is still Catherine's husband or not.

7th August 1530

Wolsey has recovered from his illness now. Although he signed the petition to the Pope, there is a rumour about that he is in fact supporting Chapuys in his demands that Henry shall return to Catherine. When Anne heard of this, her lips narrowed to a tight line, and her black eyes were hard and determined. She said nothing, but I fear that Wolsey's effort to obey both his conscience and his king may have terrible results. Anne is determined, and she is utterly unforgiving.

22nd September 1530

Rosanna has had her baby! Mama's letter says it is a little boy, and he is well and strong, God be thanked. They are going to call him John. I think of Papa, who used to be known as Mr John by the English who could not get their tongues round Michel Valjean. He would have been so proud of his grandson. I cannot wait to see my little nephew, but wait I must, at least until Christmas, when I hope we will be together.

24th October 1530

My suspicions about Anne's intentions were dreadfully right. Cardinal Wolsey's physician has made a wild accusation about his master. He says Wolsey is secretly urging the Pope to excommunicate Henry and hand the rule of England over to Queen

Catherine. We are all sure the man was bribed to tell such a story, and knowing glances are exchanged. Nobody has forgotten Anne's boast of how much she would spend to achieve Wolsey's downfall.

The King is deeply shocked. Can his old friend really be plotting against him? He paces about in scowling silence, unsure what to believe. Anne, of course, insists that the story is true. She sits beside him with her slim hand on his embroidered sleeve, whispering in his ear that Wolsey has planned this as a way to his own power, seeing himself as adviser to Catherine once Henry is deposed. "My lord," I heard her say, "you must protect yourself."

She looks impeccably concerned and serious, but I wonder what she is really thinking. Is it just a game to her, a sort of human chess where people may be deployed like pieces on a board, or does she understand that she is dealing with powerful and dangerous men? She obviously thinks she can persuade Henry to do whatever she wants, and at the moment this may be true – but it may not remain so. He adored Catherine for all the years of their happy marriage, and perhaps secretly still does, but he is ruthless in trying to rid himself of her now that his needs have changed. But Anne is a gambler, playing her game for the highest possible stakes. I sometimes wonder if she loves the danger more than she loves the King.

1st November 1530

My lady Anne has won. Today Henry drew up a warrant for the arrest of Cardinal Wolsey. By a strange irony, it will be carried out by Henry Percy, now the Earl of Northumberland, the young suitor who sought Anne's hand seven years ago and was dismissed by Wolsey. Truly, the lady's vengeance will be sweet to her. Percy has been chosen as the arresting officer, and I wonder if this was by her request. He leaves today for Cawood, in Yorkshire, to charge the Cardinal with high treason. And the punishment for that is death.

28th November 1530

Cardinal Wolsey will not have to face the humiliations of imprisonment and trial. He was a very sick man when Percy arrested him. One of the soldiers in the party said the Cardinal could hardly sit upright on his mule as they started on the long journey back to London. They had to keep stopping to do what they could to revive him, and by the time they reached Leicester it was obvious that he was dying. They sought refuge at the abbey there, and the monks tended Wolsey devotedly, but he died that night.

The King was grieved to hear the news. "I wish he had lived," he said.

What a strange man he is. How could he wish his old friend to have lived when he had just ordered his arrest and almost certain death on the scaffold? Henry always seems able to be two men at once, both the soft-hearted romantic and the ruthless despot.

Anne has no regrets, of course – quite the contrary. She laughed in triumph, and at once started planning an elaborate masque entitled *The Going to Hell of Cardinal Wolsey*. Many of us find the idea distasteful, but nobody dares say so.

21st December 1530

Once again we are at Greenwich for Christmas. I like this place so much better than Anne's palace at Whitehall. A grassy hill slopes down to the river, and Tom and I walk among the tall trees where the herons nest. Queen Catherine has joined us for Christmas, so my family is together again. It is lovely to see Mama, and the boys who both look so much bigger now. Daniel is twelve, a stocky boy, much more likeable than he was when we were children, and William has filled out and lost his paleness. I was especially delighted to see Rosanna and Diego and baby John. He is a beautiful child, with a mop of dark hair like the rest of us. I used to hold William when he was small, but I had forgotten how solid and how charged with life a baby feels. The little legs kick so strongly, and the fists wave in the air with excitement, ready to grab at a finger. Rosanna insisted on feeding him herself, though the other ladies were surprised. Most of them hand their children to a wet nurse. I would not want to do that. How does the baby ever know who his true mother is if another woman feeds him? But then children of the aristocracy have to get used to accepting things. They will have little choice about where they are sent or to whom they are married.

I thought it might be embarrassing for the Queen to be here with Henry and Anne, but the King treats his wife with great courtesy. He has her beside him at mealtimes and in the evenings to watch the masques and dancing. She looks pale and unwell, but she holds her head high, every inch the queen. It is good to have her here, in her rightful place. I do not have much chance to see her, as I have to wait on Madam Anne, who keeps mostly to her own chambers, but the warmth of Catherine's presence imbues the whole palace, and makes everyone feel more festive.

Christmas Day 1530

I shall remember this day for ever. As we walked across the frosty grass this morning, Tom asked me to marry him. He has been worried ever since Lord Rochford made his unwelcome approach to me. "If his lordship should set his mind on you instead of his shrewish wife, my objections would count for nothing," he said. "And if the King can divorce a wife he no longer wants, who is to say Rochford may not do likewise?"

We will have to ask the King's permission to marry. We both know he may not approve of one of Anne's ladies choosing a blacksmith as her husband, and I can only pray that he is in a good humour. I cannot imagine what we will do if he refuses.

27th December 1530

Tom and I were admitted to the King's presence this afternoon. I had hoped Queen Catherine would be with him, but she was not. We both knelt before him, and he listened to our request. Then he gave a bark of laughter. "Marry?" he said. "Aye, why not." He took a great draught from the cup of wine he held. "All the world seeks to marry." I could see that he was a little drunk, and felt glad of it, for wine usually improves his mood. Then he became more serious, and laid his hand first on Tom's head then mine. "Go with my blessing," he said. "Be married, by permission of your King."

I wept with gratitude and kissed his hand, and he laughed. "These are early days for tears," he said. "Those come later." His face clouded and he waved us away. "Go, leave me." And from loving him for his generosity, I once again found him alarming.

12th January 1531

We were married yesterday in the chapel here at Whitehall. The King was not present and neither was Anne, but Queen Catherine came, which gave me great joy. Mama was there, and my brothers, scrubbed and tidy and in their best clothes, and Rosanna and Diego and little John. All my friends in the court were there as well, and Chapuys came, perhaps because I am related to a previous Spanish ambassador. I only wished Papa could have lived to see this day. I almost wept as I thought of him standing at my side, and Tom understood. His hand tightened over mine, and I managed to smile. Papa would have liked Tom – he always preferred the company of "practical men", as he called them.

There was a splendid dinner for us all afterwards. I was amazed, because I know I am not one of Anne's favourite ladies. One or two of them looked at me with a curl of the lip, but most of them were at least polite, if not downright admiring of my handsome husband. I heard someone whisper, "What a lovely couple they make!" And that is true. We are a couple, and we will love each other for ever.

Tom and I will have our own room now, in whatever house or palace my lady Anne occupies. We are man and wife. *Man and wife*. I say the words again and again. I am Elinor Freeman, a married woman.

21st January 1531

King Henry has a new adviser, Thomas Cromwell. He used to be in the service of Cardinal Wolsey, but he came to court some years ago and he has now replaced the Cardinal as the King's most favoured man. He has a heavy face and small eyes that remind me of a pig. There is a mean, shrewd look about him that frightens me. He was a mercenary soldier in Italy in his younger years, fighting on the side of whichever army paid him best, and I feel he is still capable of doing whatever he is asked to do, with no scruples. Coupled with the clever and calculating Thomas Cranmer, Henry now has formidable men on his side.

24th January 1531

We hear that the Pope has at last acted. He has sent a message to King Henry, commanding him to separate himself from Anne Boleyn and return to his lawful wife. It is too late. The King was not even angry. He just laughed.

7th February 1531

Today Henry went to Parliament and told them the Church in England would no longer answer to the rule of the Pope. Instead it would have the ruling monarch as its supreme head. I thought it was an outrageous proposal, and said English people would never accept it. Tom laughed. Nobody will object, he says. The monasteries and convents will be set against it, for without the backing of Rome they will lose much of their wealth and power – but why should ordinary people mind? Tom thinks they will like the idea that they can worship God and be aware of His divine will without the intercession of the priest. And he for one is all in favour of it.

Can Tom be right? I feel guilty for even thinking about it, as if God sees the doubt in my mind and may punish me. But the daffodils are starting to bloom and the birds sing in the lengthening days, and there is no sign yet of divine retribution. Perhaps it is true that the human soul can reach God without an appointed churchman to open the way. I can see why people might find the idea exciting. But no, I must not be tempted. In my heart of hearts, I know it is sinful.

11th February 1531

King Henry's proposal has been accepted. Archbishop Warham announced today that the Act separating the Church of England from Rome has been passed, "as far as the law of Christ allows".

They say the Archbishop looked distressed as he made the announcement. Madam Anne is ecstatic, needless to say. Now that the rules have been rewritten, I suppose it is only a matter of time before Henry's divorce goes through and she becomes queen.

John Fisher, Bishop of Rochester, who defended the Queen at the Westminster hearing, says it is against God's law for a king to declare himself head of the Church. He is a brave man – and perhaps a foolish one. I was with Anne when she heard what he had said, and although she made no comment, her thin eyebrows rose over her black, beady eyes, and her lips set into their thin line of determination.

21st February 1531

I did not realize just what danger John Fisher was in. Yesterday everyone in his household collapsed at the table in terrible pain after eating the soup. Several of them are dead. Fisher himself had taken only a spoonful or two, but he was seized with agonizing stomach cramps. He is still very ill, as are the other survivors. The cook, Richard Rouse, has been arrested and accused of putting a poisonous white powder into the soup, but nobody believes the man did this of his own accord, if he did it at all. Quite clearly someone was bribed. And where did the poison come from? I hardly dare write the name. It is whispered that the powder was supplied by Lord Wiltshire. And he, of course, is Anne Boleyn's father.

We dare not guess whether the King was party to the plot to poison Fisher. He is determined to show his disapproval, so he has ordered a new punishment for poisoners. They are to be boiled alive. The unfortunate cook, Richard Rouse, is to suffer this terrible death.

8th March 1531

We are still at Greenwich, and the Queen remains part of the household, though there is constant gossip about when and how the royal divorce will take place. I think the King still hopes he may persuade Catherine to agree to a peaceful annulment of the marriage, for he goes to see her in her chambers from time to time, even though Anne throws a furious tantrum whenever he does. He looks aggrieved, and seems to be playing the part of a man forced by the need for an heir to separate from the wife he loves. And who knows, perhaps in some corner of his heart he does love Catherine still. At the same time, though, he is impatient to marry Anne.

Princess Mary is ill, and Catherine has begged the King to be allowed to go and see her in Wales. He said she could go by all means, but he added darkly, "and stay there". Mama heard the Queen's quiet answer. "I would not leave you for my daughter or for anyone else in the world." How steadfast she is, and how brave!

25th March 1531

The King relented. As Queen Catherine will not leave him, even for her daughter's sake, he sent for Princess Mary to come from Ludlow to London. Her procession arrived yesterday. She is very ill, but she survived the long journey and is now lodged at Richmond Palace. Henry allowed the Queen to join her there, and of course Mama went with her, for she will never be parted from Catherine. Rosanna and the others remain here.

19th April 1531

Mary's health is much improved now, and Catherine has come back to Greenwich, leaving her daughter in the care of Lady Salisbury.

A messenger from the Pope arrived a few days ago. He told the King his case can only be tried in Rome, and he may be excommunicated if he persists in making himself head of a separate English Church. Henry snorted with contempt. "I care not a fig for his excommunications!" he said.

4th May 1531

Queen Catherine asked Henry if Mary could come and join the court at Greenwich, but he was in one of his most irritable moods, and refused.

31st May 1531

A deputation of more than 30 peers and councillors went to see the Queen today and pleaded with her to give up her marriage. She sent them away, but not until she had told them the truth as she saw it. Mama heard what she said, and wrote it down while it was fresh in her mind. I am putting the words in this diary, because they are so brave:

I love and have loved my lord the King as much as any woman can love a man, but I would not have borne him company as his wife for one moment against the voice of my conscience. I am his true wife. Go to Rome and argue with others than a lone woman!

Henry was bellowing with rage when the deputation came back to his quarters. He said he never wanted to see Catherine again. As far as he is concerned, the marriage is over. Although I love the Queen, and admire her courage, I begin to wish she could accept what has happened. If she would give in, things would be so much better for her. Out of gratitude if nothing else, Henry would be kind to her. As it is, she refuses to accept any judgement except that of the Pope, and she is turning herself into her husband's enemy.

We are shortly moving to Windsor, so once again I am busy packing.

23rd June 1531

The King was unexpectedly kind, and allowed Princess Mary to come with us, as well as Catherine. The stay at Windsor will only be a short one, however, as we are due to move to Woodstock on the 14th of next month. After that, I suppose we will set out on summer progress, for these great houses are grimy and stinking after the winter, and in great need of their summer cleaning.

14th July 1531

We were woken in the early dawn yesterday, and told to get ready at once, as we were leaving for Woodstock. It was hardly light, but we started to carry things down to the stable yard at the back of the palace, getting ready to start out. I could see no sign of

Mama or Rosanna, but I assumed they were helping the Queen to get ready. I had not seen either of them for two or three days, as I had been so busy in Anne's quarters, sorting and packing clothes. Then Rosanna appeared, and stared in surprise at the horses and pack-mules being harnessed and the baggage being loaded. She was carrying little John because he had woken her for his early feed. She would not have heard us otherwise, for the Queen's household has its rooms on the far side of the castle, where the clatter and jingle of our preparations would not penetrate.

"I must tell Mama!" she said in alarm. "Nobody told us we were leaving so early."

The Duke of Suffolk heard her, and shook a warning finger. "Say nothing," he warned her. "Go back to bed."

She and I stared at each other, each of us understanding what the King had planned. Queen Catherine was to be left behind, without so much as a farewell. This was the final parting.

"Oh, Rosanna," I said, "when will I see you again?"

She shook her head. Neither of us knew.

We hugged each other.

"The poor queen," Rosanna whispered, and both of us wept.

A horn was blown and a man shouted the order to mount and move off. Tom waved from where he had been helping to hitch up the baggage carts, and called me to join him.

I so much wanted to run through the palace and at least say goodbye to Mama, but there was no time. Tom was on his horse now and clattering towards me, leading the bay mare I was to ride. I mounted, and turned in the saddle to touch Rosanna's hand for a last time, then we were moving across the yard and out into the lane. King Henry went past, spurring his black horse to the front of the line, and I saw that his face was set in grim determination.

I keep thinking of Queen Catherine waking to find everyone gone, with only her attendants left in that great, empty palace.

29th July 1531

I heard from Mama today for the first time since that dawn departure. She says the King sent a messenger to

Catherine yesterday, telling her she must remove herself and her staff from Windsor. The Queen must have realized in that moment that Henry has truly left her, but even then, she kept her dignity. "Go where I may, I still remain his wife," she told the man, "and for him I will pray." She was grieved that he had left without saying goodbye, she added, and hoped he was well.

I understand now why there was such an outburst of fury from the King's chambers when the man came back from Windsor and went in to see him. We could hear Henry bellowing, "I want no more of her messages!"

He tries to brush her off, but she clings as cobwebs do to velvet, and the harder he brushes, the more closely she twines herself round his fingers.

6th October 1531

I am going to have a baby. It will be born in June of next year. I am so pleased. Tom is torn between joy and anxiety, but I tell him to have faith. Many women die in childbirth, it is true, but far more do not. Look at all the people who walk about on this earth, I told him. Each one of them has been born of some woman. And I am strong and healthy. I must admit, though, the days of being on summer progress were tiresome, as I often felt so sick and queasy. I have not told the Lady Anne my news. She is full of plans for her wedding, and has little interest in anything else. During any spare moments we have been busy cutting and stitching new clothes for her.

In the weeks of moving about there has been no news of Catherine, but I had a letter from Rosanna yesterday, saying that the Queen and her attendants are now at a place called Easthampstead. Princess Mary has been sent to Richmond. I suppose the King has realized he will never persuade Catherine to give him a divorce, but none of us can imagine what he will do about it now.

27th October 1531

Mama writes to say Catherine's court has now removed to The More, a manor house in Hertfordshire that was once owned by Cardinal Wolsey. It is a pleasant place, she says, well furnished and with fine parklands surrounding it. The Queen has been granted more servants, and at the end of this month, 30 Venetians are to visit her from Italy. Mama and her other ladies are frantically preparing for them, but I am glad they are seeing some life there. I was afraid the Queen was to be banished to a life of boredom and isolation. But then of course this visit will have been planned for a long time. Henry cannot have it said that he is failing in hospitality, and neither does he want people to say he is treating his royal wife badly.

We are busy at Ely Place in the City of London, preparing for a great banquet on 10th November, but Anne continually nags us to work harder at making her new clothes. I am sick of the sight of silks and velvets and tiny pearls to be stitched in intricate patterns on bodices and collars. She knows now that I am pregnant, but when I told her she merely said, "Are you, indeed." Other people's pregnancies annoy her, for she cannot wait to be the King's wife and give him the son he so desires. She must be at least 30 now, and sometimes she looks older, when her face sets into lines of bitterness and jealousy.

Tom overheard an alarming rumour today while he was shoeing the Duke of Suffolk's horse. (It is strange how the nobility will talk to each other in front of some menial person, as though they were not being heard and understood.) Anne has warned John Fisher not to attend the next session of Parliament, lest he should suffer a repeat of the stomach pains that almost killed him in February. Fisher refuses to support the King in his new control of the Church, and Thomas More agrees with him. More is one of Henry's oldest friends, but I wonder if even he is safe.

The King is in a constant state of fury these days. He is having trouble with an old injury to his leg, sustained during a joust some years ago. It has become infected and is very painful, so he has even less patience than usual. Last summer's progress annoyed him, for the people who stood along the roadsides were still shouting that they wanted to see Catherine, their rightful queen. He is angry with them, but he cannot force them to take Anne to their hearts. And, worst of all, the bishops and the parliament seem reluctant to take the final step of declaring the royal marriage null and void. Perhaps they are not sure how to do it. After all, such a thing has never happened before, in all the long history of England.

11th November 1531

The banquet at Ely Place was staged yesterday, for all the most important men in the City of London. I suppose this had been planned for a long time, before the King and Queen parted, but the occasion really was a very strange one. Since Henry now refuses to appear in public with his wife, he entertained half the guests in one hall and she the other half in another. The royal pair did not meet throughout the whole afternoon.

When Catherine left Ely Place to return to The More, a great crowd was standing outside to cheer her and shout their support, and this did not improve the

King's temper. He is particularly furious at the moment because the Pope, after all these years of indecision, has summoned him to Rome for his case to be decided. One of the gentlemen ushers caught a glimpse of the papal document, and gleefully told us all of the words that caught his eye. They said Henry was to remove "that diabolic woman" from his bed and restore his rightful wife.

This makes everyone smile, for we all know that Anne, even yet, is not in the King's bed. With iron determination, she is waiting for marriage and the crown.

25th November 1531

A frightening thing happened last night. Anne Boleyn set out from here to dine with friends at a house by the Thames, being carried in a litter and accompanied by a small group of friends and servants, including myself. We had not gone far when a breathless man came running to warn us that a crowd was approaching – and sure enough, a multitude of women came pouring out of every street and converged on us, screaming abuse at Anne and trying to drag her from her litter. I was sure they meant to kill her and perhaps all of us. I was thrown into utter panic, not so much for Anne as for myself. In that awful moment, I could only think of the child growing inside me, and I was terrified that this small life might perish along with my own. Some of the creatures in the crowd, I could see, were men dressed as women, but they were all screaming that Anne must not be Henry's queen, and should be done away with.

Thanks to the warning, we were already heading fast for the river, and by great good fortune we were able to scramble aboard a barge and cast off with none of us harmed, but Anne was sobbing with panic, and all of us were very scared.

It is not only the common people who dislike Madam Boleyn. Her supporters at court are beginning to waver. She is so impatient with the King and speaks to him so impertinently that even her own uncles are embarrassed by her behaviour. She has upset the Dukes of Suffolk and Norfolk, and Sir Henry Guildford, who was Comptroller of the King's Household, has resigned his office and left the court, being deeply offended by something she said to him.

25th December 1531

For the first time ever, Henry has not invited the Queen to join us at court for Christmas, and the celebrations here seemed muted in her absence. Catherine sent him a gold cup, but he scowled when he received it, and gave orders that it should be returned. By contrast, he gave Anne a room hung with embroidered satin and cloth of gold. My lady, for all her tantrums, can still do no wrong.

Tomorrow she goes on a visit to her parents at Hever, and Tom and I have to be among those who go with her. It will only be a short visit, however.

8th January 1532

We are back at court in Greenwich. Anne has been installed in the chambers that used to be Catherine's.

It is so strange to look round these familiar rooms, where I used to play and sing for that great lady, and tell stories to make her laugh. There is not much laughter here now, and what there is tends to be mocking or triumphant. It is seldom simply amused.

10th January 1532

Sir Thomas More has resigned from his office of Lord Chancellor. The whole court is agog that such an old friend of the King should desert him. Sir Thomas has never approved of Anne, and he was shocked to hear that Henry will not go to Rome for the Pope's judgement. Remembering what happened to Wolsey, I wondered if the King would order More's arrest, but he seemed saddened rather than angry. He is allowing his old friend to retire to his quiet house at Chelsea. At least for now.

25th January 1532

Henry has proclaimed that he is permitting Princess Mary to visit her mother at Enfield. He ordered this to be made widely known, and we can all see why. The people know now that Catherine spent Christmas on her own, and they mutter against the King for his bad treatment of his royal wife and daughter. For this reason, he is more than usually anxious to be seen as just and generous.

Today I felt the child inside me begin to move – just a small flutter, but I know it is alive and well. Anne Boleyn gives me more work to do than ever before, but the other women help me. I feel almost sorry for her. She is almost double my age, and she must be wondering if she will ever have a baby of her own.

23rd April 1532

King Henry is having increasing trouble with his subjects. On Easter Sunday, with the King and Anne before him in the church at Greenwich, Friar William Peto had the incredible boldness (and courage) to preach against Anne Boleyn. He warned Henry that if he made an "unlawful" marriage with the woman who sat beside him, God would punish him as He had punished Ahab, and the dogs would lick his blood. The King turned purple with rage, and he walked out of the church with Anne hurrying at his heels. They say Peto is to be banished from the kingdom.

19th May 1532

Princess Mary's visit to her mother may well be her last, it seems. Mama writes from The More to say the Queen has been ordered to have no further contact with her daughter. Catherine has to leave The More and move to a place called Bishop's Hatfield, in Hertfordshire. She will miss Mary dreadfully. I am sure her loyal servants will carry messages between the two of them, but it is a sad thing all the same.

Meanwhile, the King is spending huge amounts of money on resplendent new clothes for Anne. Her requirements are far more than we can make here, so other dressmakers are at work. She has a gown of gold-embroidered velvet that cost £74, she boasts, and her latest order is for a black satin gown lined with black velvet, to be worn in her bedchamber if she chooses to receive guests there.

13th June 1532

The bishops are still deeply troubled at the idea of breaking away from Rome, and they understand very clearly that all this is happening because Henry wants to take a new wife. John Fisher preached against the union with Anne last week, and we all thought the King would be furious, but he shrugged it off. He has been much occupied, they say, in drawing up a new pact of friendship with France.

The whole thing is exhausting to think about. I often wish I could be in some other place, where life could be simple and straightforward. I am not often so tired and out of sorts, but the coming child makes me feel burdened and heavy.

2nd July 1532

Last week, on 26th June, my beautiful son was born. His name is Michael, after my father's French name of Michel, and he is strong and healthy. I am sorely exhausted, for the birth took a long time, but Tom cares for me well, and my friends among the court servants bring me small treats of beef and venison, with wine to build up my strength. How ironic it is that Tom and I have produced this boy child with no more than ordinary pain, while the King is tearing the country apart in his desperation to have a son.

28th August 1532

The summer progress did not last long this year. I was excused from going because my baby is so young, but Tom had to be with them, so I am selfishly glad the journeying was cut short. He says the crowds were so hostile to Anne that the King lost his temper and commanded a return to London. The servants are in a terrible panic because the cleaning is not finished.

The King's anger has reached out to touch Catherine, I suppose, because he hates the way she still has the people's support. A letter from Mama today says he has dismissed Maria de Salinas (now Lady Willoughby) from the Queen's service. It is a cruel thing to do, for Maria is Catherine's oldest friend. Mama, too, will miss her, for she was one of the original Spanish ladies, one of the few left in the Queen's household.

Old Archbishop Warham died last week. Henry does not bother to pretend any regret, for Warham was one of Catherine's most loyal supporters. Thomas Cranmer will be the new Archbishop of Canterbury, and he, of course, is firmly on the side of the King…

30th August 1532

Someone left a book of prophecies in Anne Boleyn's apartments, and the lady found in it a crudely drawn picture of herself with her head cut off. I was with her when she opened the book. For a moment she stared at the picture as if in perplexity, but then she tossed it aside and said it was a mere bauble. She certainly has courage. I would have been terribly upset to find such a thing – and frightened, too.

The King is determined to suppress any hostility towards his chosen queen. A man called Thomas Abell was sent to the Tower last week for publicly criticizing Anne, and people say he is not the only one.

1st September 1532

Today, with much ceremony, King Henry made Anne Boleyn a peeress in her own right, here at Windsor. She is now the Marquess of Pembroke, a title never before given to a woman.

I listened carefully to the words the herald read out in the grand chamber as Anne knelt before the King. There was reference to the title being handed on to any child Anne might bear, but a glance ran round as it was said, and eyebrows were raised. I wondered why, and made a note to ask someone later.

Henry placed a gold coronet on Anne's head and draped the crimson velvet mantle of state about her shoulders, then raised her to her feet as the trumpets sounded.

Apparently the phrase about inheriting the title usually contains the words "*lawfully begotten* offspring". This time, these words had been omitted. To talk of offspring that are perhaps not lawfully begotten can only mean one thing. Madam Boleyn has at last allowed the King into her bed, and he knows she may be pregnant.

Since Michael was born, I have not been serving Anne in her chambers. She dismissed me impatiently when I came back, saying I would be more useful with a needle than with a chamber pot. I knew I irked her with my full bosom and my absences every few hours to go and feed my baby. I reminded her too sharply of the child Henry so desperately wants. So I have been stitching at her new regal clothes instead, and have only the words of the other ladies to tell me what has been happening. Or not happening.

As everyone knows, a virgin girl will bleed a little when a man first makes love to her – but the ladies swear that Anne's sheets bore no stain. This titbit of gossip ran round the court like wildfire, and everyone is secretly laughing. No wonder the Lady Boleyn held out for all these years, they say. The King would have cooled very rapidly once he knew he was not her first lover.

If Henry is disappointed, he shows no sign of it. He seems full of good cheer, and takes an obvious delight in his royal mistress, constantly letting his hand rest over hers and exchanging a private smile with her. And of course he would look extremely foolish should he try to discard her now. After these years of turmoil on her behalf, he can hardly say he made a mistake.

There is soon to be a meeting with King Francis in France. A large royal party will be going, so we are thrown into the usual fever of preparation.

6th September 1532

An embarrassing difficulty has occurred. No French lady can be found who is willing to accept Anne Boleyn as a guest. Queen Eleanor refuses to do so, and so does the French king's sister, now Queen of Navarre, who has described Anne's behaviour as "the scandal of Christendom". I do not know what is to happen. Henry will not go without Anne, but he cannot take her unless proper arrangements can be made.

10th September 1532

Anne has demanded that Queen Catherine shall hand over her jewels so that she, Anne, may wear them during her visit to France. I know the Queen will refuse, for these are the jewels of state, for only a reigning queen to wear — but if Henry sends her a written order to comply with the request, she will have to obey.

Henry, meanwhile, obeys Anne. Because of her objections, he now hardly ever goes to see his daughter, Princess Mary, whom he loves. Last week, Anne threatened to bring Mary here to be one of her serving women. And then she added, with a laugh that chilled me, that she might give the princess "too much dinner". We all remember what happened at John Fisher's dinner table, and there can be no doubt what the lady meant. Mary is safer to stay away from this court.

6th October 1532

Tomorrow we depart for Dover, the King and Madam Anne, with a great train of attendants. My lady has insisted that I must accompany her, although she knows I do not want to leave my baby for a trip that will take several weeks. I cannot disobey, of course. Tom has to come as well. Little Michael is almost weaned, which is just as well, and the woman looking after him assures me he will be well cared for. I know this is true, but I am still wretched at the thought of going so far away and handing my son to somebody else. I never used to be afraid for myself, but I am full of terrors now. What if the ship sinks? What if I fall prey to some terrible foreign disease and never come back to see him again? But there is no help for it – I have to go.

No hostess was found for Anne Boleyn, so she and Henry will stay at the Exchequer Palace in Calais, which belongs to England. Anne will remain there while Henry goes on to meet with Francis in the French kingdom.

14th November 1532

I did not take my diary with me to France. There is much in it that I would not like Anne Boleyn's supporters to see, and on such a journey who could know whether personal things would be kept safe from prying eyes?

It took us three days to reach Dover. The Nun of Kent was waiting for us at Canterbury. Her worldly name is Elizabeth Barton, they tell me, and she has been prophesying doom for Anne and the King for years. She seemed a little mad, I thought. She began ranting against Anne, prophesying that King Henry would come to disaster if he went on keeping her company, and I was surprised that he did not have her arrested. Anne Boleyn's mother, the Countess of Wiltshire, suggested that Anne should make the Nun one of her serving women, thus forcing her to behave herself. Someone offered the post to the woman, but she turned it down with contempt and disgust, so I fear Elizabeth Barton has sealed her own fate. Thomas Cromwell, who was with us until we took ship, said he would deal with the matter, and his small, piggy eyes held a look of relish at the prospect.

We crossed to France in a ship called *The Swallow*. The voyage took seven hours, and I was wretchedly sick. I began to fear I would never see land again, so it was a great relief to me when we came to Calais. Various dignitaries met us there, and the inevitable welcoming speeches were made. Then they escorted us to the Exchequer Palace, and ushered Anne and the King to their communicating rooms.

There was feasting and merry-making for over a week, then on Friday morning Henry rode out of Calais to meet with the French king. He came back four days later, bringing King Francis and a great retinue to be entertained as his guests. Anne did not go down to greet them, and made no appearance during the following day. She stayed in her rooms for the whole of Saturday and most of Sunday, planning her grand entrance. During that time we were working hard, making masks and getting elegant clothes ready for Anne and ourselves.

We stayed upstairs on the Sunday night until the supper things had been cleared, then seven of us followed Anne down the great stairs. We looked very striking, I suppose, in our most gorgeous gowns and our jewelled and embroidered masks, and Anne herself was resplendent in cloth of gold slashed with crimson satin. Her sleeves were of silver cloth, bound with gold cords. With her slim figure and her dark hair laced with strings of seed pearls, I must admit, she looked magnificent. She walked boldly across to King Henry, extended her hand to him and asked him to dance, and the pair of them took the floor. The rest of us chose other gentlemen as our partners, and the revelry began. As the evening went on, King Henry pretended great surprise in taking off our masks and discovering who we were. For all his ferocity, he is still a boy when it comes to music and entertainment.

The French king left Calais two days later, but by then he had spoken several times with the Lady Anne, and seemed delighted with her. After he had gone, we stayed on for a fortnight longer, for no purpose but pleasure and amusement. I suppose Henry and his beloved were on a kind of honeymoon. We busied ourselves in packing all the things we could, ready for when calm weather should return. For days on end, the sea was impossibly rough.

On Tuesday 11th November, we heard that the wind was set fair for England, so we sailed to Dover.

This time, the crossing was easier, and my queasy stomach was soothed by the knowledge that Tom and I would soon be with our little son again. And, thank the Lord, he seems no worse for the parting.

Christmas 1532

Rumour has it that Anne Boleyn is pregnant. We wait to hear whether this is true.

9th January 1533

Anne Boleyn is indeed expecting a child. We are all in a flutter of excitement, wondering what the King will do now. He is still married to Queen Catherine, but he will be desperate to marry Ann and legitimize the coming heir – they say he is sure the baby will be a boy. Can he really take a second wife? It seems utterly illegal to me, but perhaps King Henry can make his own laws now.

25th January 1533

I woke before dawn this morning because Michael was crying. I picked him up and stood rubbing his back to ease him – and I could hear that people were moving about somewhere in the royal chambers. There was the thud of a muffled door and the murmur of voices, and after a little while an incantation of Latin began, with responses from a man's voice and then a woman's. My spine prickled in the darkness, for I was sure I was hearing a marriage service. The King's private chapel opens from his own quarters below our room in this palace of Whitehall.

When the baby quietened, I tucked him back into his cradle and crept back to cuddle in beside Tom. He was awake, too, and we murmured together, sharing our suspicion that Anne Boleyn was becoming a second wife to the King.

It was morning when we woke again. We set about the work of the day, and nothing was said by anyone of what had happened before dawn – and yet I caught a glance exchanged between Lady Berkeley and Anne Savage which made me certain they shared a secret knowledge. If there was indeed a marriage ceremony, Anne Boleyn would be attended by at least two ladies – and these two would be the most likely, being her favourites. No doubt we will hear the truth when it suits the King to announce it.

5th February 1533

Anne Boleyn cannot resist boasting about her pregnancy, though it is still supposed to be a secret. In front of a large group of courtiers, she told Thomas Wyatt, the poet, she had an insatiable craving for apples. The King had told her this was a sign of pregnancy, she added, but of course it could be no such thing. And she laughed. Thomas Wyatt was once in love with Anne himself, but those days are long gone. He looked embarrassed by what she said. One of the serving men overheard him telling Chapuys that he felt ashamed of her, I suppose to make it clear that he no longer has any liking for Anne. Chapuys will no doubt pass this on to the Queen, whom he devotedly supports.

18th February 1533

A letter from Mama brought bad news today. The King has ordered Queen Catherine to move her small household to Ampthill, a house she has visited many times as a royal wife and head of the court. Now she will be sent there with no company but her few attendants, and the place is quite far from London. Mama says the poor lady feels she has been banished, and this seems very true. She spent a wretched Christmas alone, and she is far from well.

I am sure King Henry piles on these hardships in the hope that Catherine will give in and agree to an annulment of her marriage. Had she done this when he first asked, he would most probably have treated her well and continued to visit her. In fact, at times when Madam Boleyn was being temperamental and impatient, Henry might have been glad to return to the arms of a loving and ever-tolerant wife. But Catherine is the daughter of a warrior queen, Isabella of Spain, and her pride will never allow her to give in. She has told Mama many times that she would rather die than have her marriage to Henry considered illegal.

25th February 1533

There was a great banquet here last night. The King was behaving like a young bridegroom, kissing Anne before the whole company, and carousing with his friends. As the evening went on, he became very drunk. He was roaring with laughter and pouring out incoherent words, but we all grasped what he meant when he swept an arm round the great hall with its sumptuous hangings and its tables resplendent with gold plate, and said what a rich marriage his sweetheart had made. *Had made*. Eyebrows were raised as those who were still sober glanced at each other. The secret is out now. Henry and Anne are indeed married. The King has two wives.

8th April 1533

Anne's brother, Viscount Rochford, has been away for three weeks in France, on a secret mission. We all guessed that he went to tell the French king of Henry's marriage and Anne's pregnancy, and I think we were probably right. Rochford returned yesterday, and was closeted with Henry for a long time – and today the King made the official announcement that he has married Anne Boleyn and that she carries the royal heir. He appointed the Dukes of Norfolk and Suffolk to break the news to Queen Catherine, and they have already left for Ampthill.

11th April 1533, Good Friday

Archbishop Cranmer has asked the King for formal permission to judge on the question of annulling his marriage to Catherine. I cannot see by what authority the Archbishop can take it on himself to give a ruling – but I suppose everything is different, now the King no longer respects the word of the Pope.

13th April 1533, Easter Sunday

Yesterday, Anne Boleyn went in grand procession with King Henry to hear Mass. She was sumptuously gowned and decked with the jewels, and 60 of us accompanied her, all dressed in our silks and velvets. The whole court was uneasy at this parading of her before the public as Henry's new queen. How can she truly be queen when Henry is still married to Catherine? There is a terrible shamelessness about it. Anne's slender body shows the thickness of her pregnancy very clearly, and she glories in it. The people stared at her in silence as she passed, then muttered among themselves.

The King was obviously nettled by this continued public dislike. On return from Mass, he demanded that we all respect his lady as Queen of England, and says she will be crowned on Whit Sunday, 1st June.

This evening he read out the names of those who will form part of Anne's royal household. Her uncle, Sir James Boleyn, will be chancellor, and another relative, William Cosyn, her Master of Horse. I am to be among her ladies, and so is Anne Saville. Others include the Lady's cousin, Madge Shelton, Anne Gainsford, Lady Berkeley, Jane Seymour and Elizabeth Holland, who is the mistress of another of Anne's uncles, the Duke of Norfolk.

I quake inwardly to think of what would happen should Henry's new queen guess how much I detest the idea of this new arrangement. I have never fawned upon her as some of the other ladies do, and wonder sometimes why she seems to like me. I can only suppose it is because I play and sing well, and can keep her amused. Or perhaps she enjoys the fact that I have to serve her, whether I like it or not.

15th April 1533

I had a letter from Mama today. She was much distressed by the visit of the Dukes of Norfolk and Suffolk last week. They told Catherine she was no longer queen, merely the Princess Dowager of Wales. Henry has agreed that she may keep her property – what remains of it – but he will not pay her servants' wages or meet her household expenses after Easter.

The King's harshness appals me, but I suppose he cannot believe that his own wife continues to defy him. She does so out of love, because she has devoted her life to him, but her love has become an iron cage to her husband now, and he would do anything to break it. How terrible that a marriage should wither away to such a bitter ghost of itself.

I heard today that a woman called Margaret Chancellor has been thrown into prison for referring to Anne as "a goggle-eyed whore". She is not the only one to say such things, though the wise take care to speak only among trusted friends.

23rd May 1533

On the 10th of this month, Cranmer brought a court of judgement together to give a final verdict on the King's case, and today the judges declared King Henry's marriage to Catherine of Aragon null and void.

So it is done at last. I knew it had to happen, but I am filled with a deep sadness. Princess Mary, we hear, faced the assembled clerics bravely, telling them she would never accept that her mother was anything other than the rightful Queen of England. Catherine herself never appeared before the court.

28th May 1533

This morning Archbishop Cranmer announced from a high gallery in Lambeth Palace that he found the King's marriage to Anne "good and valid". It was like a signal for the celebrations to start, for within a few hours Anne was on her way up the river from Greenwich to the Tower, where she will stay as custom demands until she is crowned Queen of England this coming Sunday. What a wonderful sight it was! The Lord Mayor of London and all his aldermen escorted her up the river in a multitude of boats and barges, all sumptuously equipped with awnings of cloth of gold. Banners and streamers fluttered, and the air was full of music, for bands of musicians had been crammed on to the decks of barges and played constantly. I was glad not to be among them, for it was far more fun simply to be among the ladies escorting Anne. Poor Mark Smeaton confessed to me yesterday that he was terrified he might be pushed into the water, playing in such a crowd, but I laughed and patted his shoulder. Mark is always afraid the worst will happen.

Anne sat enthroned in the royal barge, wearing a gown of silver-white tissue, and with her dark hair loose and flowing. She is visibly pregnant, of course, being six months gone, but she looked bridal all the same, and made a fitting centrepiece to the great pageant. So many boats surrounded us that they filled the river from bank to bank, all resplendent with their coloured awnings and with pennants flying. It was as if a host of brilliant butterflies had settled on the water with folded wings of purple and crimson, scarlet and silver and gold.

When we came to the Tower, there was a salvo of welcoming gunfire from the cannon that pointed their long barrels across the river, and the noise was so shattering that I clapped my hands over my ears, as did most people. Tom tells me additional guns had been brought in, so there were more than a thousand. Their combined thunder shook the air so violently that every pane of glass in the Tower and in the neighbouring buildings was broken.

The King was waiting for Anne, and as she stepped ashore at the entry to the Tower he kissed her fondly. Then he led her into the royal apartments, which have been freshly decorated and refurbished. He will stay with her there for two nights, then on Saturday he will go ahead of her to Westminster Hall, ready to receive her when she arrives in grand procession for a civic reception. The coronation itself will be on the following day.

Anne's uncle, the Duke of Norfolk, organized all these celebrations. He has done a wonderful job, being the efficient man he is, but I have seen a glance of tight-lipped disapproval on his face in recent days when he looked at his niece. People say he has not forgiven her for so shamelessly flaunting herself as the King's mistress. All the same, the Boleyn tribe must be pleased that they now hold such power in the court. Anne is able to confer immense benefits on those whom she favours. Norfolk himself has cause to be indebted to her, for his daughter married the King's natural son, Henry Fitzroy, and Anne even ensured that no dowry was demanded.

31st May 1533

Anne left the Tower this morning and was taken with great ceremony through London to meet the King at Westminster Hall. There was no lack of brilliance in the procession – it extended half a mile behind her, they say, and we were all magnificently dressed and mounted on fine horses – but the people were oddly reluctant to celebrate. It seemed they came merely to stare.

They had glorious things to stare at. Anne was carried in a litter hung with white cloth of gold, drawn by two white palfreys, and she wore her hair loose under a gold circlet studded with jewels. To shelter her, riders on either side of her carried a canopy on gold poles hung with small silver bells. The tinkling of these bells could be heard with embarrassing clarity in the silence, for the crowds lining the streets did not cheer. They should have been roistering and happy, for the public fountains ran with wine, but they remained obstinately unfestive. Few of the men even bothered to remove their caps in respect, and there was hardly a cheer.

Some of the courtiers in our procession shouted abuse at the people, berating them for their discourtesy – but then a worse thing happened. Some wit in the crowd pointed to the intertwined initials, H and A, that appeared on every banner, and shouted ironically, "HA! HA!" In the next moment dozens of other voices had taken it up, and jeering laughter rang through the London streets.

Anne was distressed and angry by the time we reached the hall in Westminster for her state reception, and I am not surprised. She has waited and worked many years for this day, and the moment of her triumph has turned sour. I have never liked her, and I disapprove of much that she has done, but today I could not help feeling sorry for her.

Sunday 1st June 1533, Coronation Day

A great train of us walked from the Hall to Westminster on this Whitsunday morning. Anne wore a purple velvet cloak over a gown of crimson velvet edged with ermine, and her hair was again flowing loose, beaded with pearls and caught by a golden coronet. Red carpeting covered our way and stretched right through the Abbey to the high altar.

Again the crowds stood in silence, few men even bothering to take off their caps. The women eyed the pregnant queen with dislike, knowing Anne and Henry were not married when the child was conceived. No common woman could parade herself through the streets in such a condition, and they do not see why "the King's whore", as she has so long been called, should now be honoured. I saw the Nun of Kent, ranting as usual on a street corner and waving her fist, and they tell me she was arrested later. I am only surprised that pig-faced Cromwell waited so long.

When it was all over, I heard Chapuys say the coronation was "a cold, meagre and uncomfortable thing", but I feel he was being a little ungenerous. The people were cold, certainly, but within Westminster Hall the banquet that followed the coronation ceremony was magnificent. Course followed course, trumpeters played, and the music and celebration was glorious. It was something of a trial for Anne herself. She sat on a high dais in full view of the revellers, but her pregnancy is putting pressure on her bladder and she needs to relieve herself frequently. Two women were hidden beneath the sumptuous cloth, and when the need arose, they lifted the Queen's skirts for her and provided a receptacle. I would not have been in their place for anything.

There are days of merriment to follow, with jousting and hunting and dancing. I will enjoy it, for with so many musicians here, my services will not be so much in demand. As a court lady attending Anne, my main duty will be to join wholeheartedly in the revels – and who could be so mean-minded as to resent such a pleasant task? I feel almost guilty, though, for Tom is not here to share in all this celebration. He is a blacksmith, not a courtier, and throughout these days he has been at home with Michael. It was not my choice to be here, and if Tom and I follow our dream of living in some small place of our own, this may be the last grand occasion I will see. "Enjoy it, my sweetheart," Tom said. "Such a thing is something to remember. You will tell your grandchildren about it." And he is right, of course.

28th June 1533

To my joy, I find I am pregnant again. Michael was a year old two days ago, and it will be good for him to have a little brother or sister. I have written to tell Mama. She is starting to pack up the Queen's belongings, for in a month's time they have to transfer to a small and reputedly damp house at Buckden, in Huntingdonshire.

Anne is of a great size now, and constantly complains that the coming baby has ruined her figure. I think she mentions this so often in order to remind everyone that she carries the King's hoped-for son.

Chapuys has been saying he fears Henry may have Catherine murdered, and perhaps Mary as well, so exasperated is he with his ex-wife's obstinacy. When given an official notice of the court's judgement on her marriage, Catherine scored out the words "Princess Dowager" that had been used to describe herself. She insists that she is still the Queen.

I think the Spanish ambassador overstates his fears. The King is so taken up with Anne and the coming child that he hardly thinks of anything else. He has made no plans to go on progress this year. We are preparing to remove Anne's household to Hampton Court, where she will rest through the summer weeks, and Henry will stay near London so he can see her when he wishes. After some weeks at Windsor, we will go to Greenwich for the actual birth.

The Nun of Kent was brought before Archbishop Cranmer a few days ago, and he released her with the warning that she must stop ranting in the streets and inciting the people. She has been lucky.

11th August 1533

Mama writes to say they have now removed to Buckden. It is in the Fen country, wild and desolate, and the house is surrounded by a moat, which increases its dampness as well as making the Queen feel cut off from the outside world. People ran beside her procession as she came to the place, calling good wishes to her and saying they would serve her and, if necessary, die for her.

Catherine has little money now, Mama says, and food is sparse, but even so the Queen often fasts throughout the day, eating nothing. She gives what coins she can spare to the poor people of the parish, and next to her skin, Mama says, she wears the hair shirt of the Order of St Francis to remind her of the dangers of arrogance and self-indulgence. She still works at her beautiful embroidery, producing altar-cloths for the churches in the district, but many hours of each day pass in prayer.

Anne has demanded that Catherine send her the christening gown that was brought from Spain. I was outraged to hear of this, for the gown is Catherine's personal property, worn by the infant Mary for her christening. Mama worked on its embroidery, together with the Queen herself. The Lady goes too far here – she cannot make Catherine give it up.

Mama's letter says the Pope has drawn up the papers to excommunicate Henry for his illegal marriage to Anne – but Catherine has begged His Holiness not to deliver them to the King. In her eyes, to be cut off from the Church and unable to share in its direct connection with God is the most terrible thing that can happen to the human soul, and she cannot bear this to happen to her husband, even though he has deliberately courted it.

18th August 1533

What a scene there was today! Anne has found out that her royal husband has been having an affair with some other lady. I don't know who it is, for we came here to Greenwich Palace just a few days ago to await the birth of the baby, and the court gossip has not reached me. It reached Madam Boleyn, however, and she is furious. She screamed at Henry and called him names, and he was equally angry. He expects his wife to settle down into the background of his life now, bearing children and putting up uncomplainingly with whatever he chooses to do.

He berated Anne, undeterred by the fact that Jane Seymour and I were in the room. He regretted giving her a magnificent French bed, he told her, and had it not just been delivered, he would have stopped the order. She must remember that she had been made queen purely by his favour, and he could humble her again whenever he chose. With that, he walked out of the room and did not come back.

I would have been in tears at such a scolding, but Anne tossed her head, and her lips were pressed tight. She seems not to realize that her trump card has been played now, and she has no more bargaining power. She has given the King what he wants, in the form of the child that waits to be born, and there is no more thrill of the chase. He will turn for his amusement to other young women now, not as potential wives but in the same spirit that he will follow a deer or a wild boar through the forest. King Henry is above all a hunter. Catherine understood this, and waited with dignity for her husband to return to her from his latest chase, which he always did until Anne refused to be caught. Henry expects Anne to do the same, but she has not realized that this is a duty of the royal wife.

That is the trouble, I suppose, with a girl who has not been brought up in aristocratic circles. For all her love of power, Anne has common instincts, much as I do. She wants a husband who truly loves her and will be faithful to her. But Anne's husband is not like my Tom. He is a king. Women are a delight to him and he loves them quite sincerely for a while, but they are part of the great game of power, and will be discarded as soon as he tires of them.

27th August 1533

The Nun of Kent has been prophesying again, despite her warning from Cranmer a month ago, and it seems she is a complete fraud! She admits now that she has never had a vision in her life. I cannot imagine they will release her this time.

29th August 1533

Anne has insisted that Princess Mary be brought here, to work in her service. It's an outrageous order. Mary is a royal princess and heir to the throne. To make her attend during the birth of the half-brother who is meant to take her place as heir is an act of pure spite, but we all understand its purpose. This will be Anne Boleyn's sweetest moment of triumph. I never thought Henry would agree to such a suggestion, but he has not forgiven Mary for defending her mother so vigorously when the divorce was announced. Anyone who stands up for Catherine now incurs his fury. Even his own daughter.

7th September 1533

Anne's labour began early this morning, and at three in the afternoon she was delivered of a healthy child – but it is a girl. If there is any triumph, it must be Princess Mary's, who now remains first in line to be the Queen of England.

The King is bitterly disappointed. He barely glanced at his new daughter, though she is a lovely baby with red-gold hair like his own. Her name will be Elizabeth.

10th September 1533

Anne is a devoted mother. She adores her baby girl, seeming unperturbed by Henry's displeasure, and wants to feed the child herself. This will not be allowed, of course. A queen does not suckle her children like a cow suckling a calf. A common woman has already been engaged as a wet nurse, and Anne will have to be content with holding her daughter at the times permitted by the pattern of the royal day. Poor thing – I would hate such interference.

The Nun of Kent has been sent to the Tower. And Bishop Fisher is under house arrest. I have not heard what the charge against him is to be, but Anne has been complaining about him ceaselessly ever since he survived the poisoned soup.

2nd October 1533

The King did not attend his daughter's christening. I hear the official announcement of the child's birth now bears a clumsy amendment because there was no space left in which to change the word, "Prince" to "Princess". This made me laugh, but Anne of course does not find it amusing. She knows I am pregnant again, and yesterday she looked at me and said, "I will not be far behind you." She has failed to produce a son this time, but at least she has survived the birth, and little Elizabeth is strong and healthy. All she can hope for is to produce another child as soon as possible, and that it will be male. Meanwhile, Henry has again been unfaithful to her, and again, Anne made a fuss. She does not learn.

4th December 1533

Anne expects a second child, she announces.

Henry has now sent little Elizabeth away to Hatfield Palace, where, at three months old, she will have her own staff and household. To be fair to him, Hatfield is a healthier place than London, with its smoke-filled and noxious air, but Anne will miss her little daughter. I feel sorry for her.

Princess Mary is to go to Hatfield as an attendant to her little half-sister. In fact, she loves the baby and cares for her devotedly, but we all know the intention is further to humiliate her. Ever since Elizabeth's birth, Anne's malice against the daughter of Queen

Catherine – or the Dowager Princess, as she is now supposed to be known – has become positively savage. Mary has been stripped of her title of Princess, and is effectively reduced to being a servant. Her household at Beaulieu is to be disbanded, and Henry is giving her manor house to Anne's brother.

10th December 1533

Henry decided to visit his little Elizabeth in Hatfield, and set out without saying anything to Anne about it. What a rumpus it caused! When the Lady found out where he had gone, she flew into a rage, convinced that his real purpose was to see Mary and perhaps make his peace with her.

Anne sent for Cromwell and commanded him to set out after the King to make sure he had no contact with Mary. Pig-face evidently did his job well, for the King's elder daughter was not to be found during the royal visit. On departing though, Henry glanced back, and saw her on a balcony. She fell on her knees to him, entreating him to stay. For a moment, the King hesitated as if inclined to turn back, regardless of Anne's wrath. He swept off his hat and bowed to Mary, and all the courtiers did likewise. But then he rode away.

We have heard since that Anne has demanded possession of all Mary's jewellery, saying that his "bastard daughter" has no right to it.

14th December 1533

Catherine has asked if she may be transferred to somewhere less damp and cold, as her health is suffering. Anne cruelly suggested she should go to Somersham, which everyone knows to be even worse than the Huntingdonshire house. Chapuys protested to Henry that this was impossible, and apparently the King smiled benignly and said she could go to Fotheringhay. Chapuys thinks he has scored a victory, but we all know Fotheringhay is even worse than Somersham, so he has done the poor lady no service. However, Henry has given his instructions, and the

Duke of Suffolk is to be sent with a detachment of the King's Guards to force Catherine to obey the order.

The Duke does not want to go. He married a young bride only three months ago, and to ride to a cold and uncivilized county in December is not at all to his liking. He told Maria de Salinas, we hear, that he hoped he and his troops would meet with some mishap on the way that would force them to return, and I am sure his soldiers agree with him.

22nd December 1533

The Duke is having a difficult time of it in Huntingdonshire. Tom spoke to the man who rode from there yesterday with a message for the King, and heard the full story. On hearing that she was to move to Fotheringhay, Catherine locked herself in her room and said he would have to break the door down if he wanted to get her out.

The Duke could not do this, obviously. After all, Catherine belongs to the most powerful royal family in

Europe. Her nephew is Charles of the Habsburgs, a warlike and domineering emperor who is quite capable of attacking any country whose ruler displeases him. We all know Henry would have been much firmer in dealing with his ex-wife, had it not been for the lurking fear that complaints from her to Charles might turn the Emperor against the English king. Mama has always said the Queen would not dream of stirring up trouble for Henry, as she adores him, but perhaps men who think only in terms of politics and power do not realize that.

Anyway, the Duke dismissed almost every member of Catherine's staff, leaving only the Spanish ones, and arrested her two chaplains for refusing to call her the Dowager Princess. The dismissed servants told the local people what was going on, and within a short time the village men were standing silently along the moat that surrounds Buckden, armed with cudgels, pitchforks and whatever other weapons came to hand.

Suffolk will not be having a very happy Christmas. And neither will I, for I worry about Mama. It will not be so bad for Rosanna, for she has Diego to help and support her. Mama, though, is deeply devoted to the Queen, and she will be so anxious and fearful. And what of my brothers? Daniel is fifteen now, and has been working in the Queen's household for quite some time. William has been making himself useful as well, since he is twelve, but neither of them has learned to speak good Spanish. Will they have been sent away? I can only wait to find out.

I hate this dark time of the year, when the days are so short and the nights so long and cold. Tom says we must look forward to the spring, when our next baby will be born – but it seems a long time away.

26th December 1533

In the middle of the feasting and merry-making, I cannot help thinking of my family and Queen Catherine, prisoners in that cold, damp house. The Duke of Suffolk and his men are still there, though none of us can see why. Perhaps they are making sure the dismissed servants do not sneak back into the building and continue to serve the Queen.

The last rider who came back said the villagers are still surrounding the house, for they love their queen, and will die in her defence if necessary. No letters have come from Rosanna or Mama. Tom says I must trust in God, for there is nothing I can do, and he is right, of course. But it is hard not to worry.

Anne's Christmas present to Henry was a great basin made entirely of gold and set with rubies and pearls. It contains a diamond-studded fountain in the form of three naked nymphs, whose nipples spout jets of water. There were cries of admiration, of course, but afterwards I heard one lady whisper to another, "My dear, did you ever see anything so vulgar?"

6th January 1534

Suffolk and his men are back from Buckden, the King having ordered their return, and my brothers are with them, thank the Lord. William has a bad cough and looks very thin and white, but Daniel is his usual robust self. The Queen has set him to work in the stables, where Tom is keeping an eye on him. He is going to teach him to shoe horses, and that will be good, for a man with a skilled trade can always earn a living. I gave William some chicken broth and put him to bed in our room, but he shivers in spite of the blankets.

The soldiers are grumbling and cursing at having spent a cold and miserable Christmas under the gaze of hostile villagers, and one of them who saw Catherine was horrified by how old and frail she looked. Suffolk himself told the King his ex-wife seems to be suffering from some serious illness, but if Henry was moved by this news, he did not show it.

The letter that one of the soldiers brought me from Mama said the house had been stripped of almost all its furniture, and the place is terribly bare and cold. The Queen's few remaining servants are all Spaniards, or at least part-Spaniards like Rosanna, and every one of them pretended to speak no English when questioned. The Bishop of Llandaff speaks Spanish, and he has been permitted to stay as Catherine's chaplain. But these things seem a scant comfort.

17th January 1534

William seems better. He ate some stewed venison today, then slept again. Daniel is very happy, working with Tom. I found him in the forge this morning, hammering a piece of red-hot iron and making the sparks fly. I wrote to Mama today to tell her the boys are both safe, and gave the letter to a rider who was carrying messages to her chaplain.

Someone has given Henry a peacock and a pelican. They are wonderful birds to look at, but they make a terrible noise, especially the peacock. Anne has complained that they disturb her sleep, so they are to be handed on to Sir Henry Norris in Greenwich. I have always liked Norris – he seems one of the nicest and most obliging of Henry's gentlemen. I hope he and his wife sleep more soundly than Lady Anne does.

23rd February 1534

Outbreaks of rebellious talk about Anne crop up everywhere. I have heard reports of people saying that Henry is living with his new queen in adultery, and Henry Percy, who once loved Anne, said openly the other day that she was "a bad woman". The King is seething with anger.

Lord Dacre has been tried for treason. We all feared for him, as he has been outspoken in his defence of Catherine, and has constantly opposed Anne. But after he had spoken for seven hours in his own defence, the jury unanimously acquitted him. This has not improved the King's temper.

William is recovered enough to start working as a kitchen boy. He has been turning the spit today, and his face was pink from the heat of the fire and the smell of the roasting meat clung to him.

23rd March 1534

Today Parliament passed the Act of Succession. It means that any subject who says or writes anything derogatory about the King and his new wife will be guilty of high treason, for which the penalty is death.

I find this very frightening. As my father's daughter I grew up in the happy assumption that all things were open to be laughed at, even if one had to be cautious about the moment chosen for the joke. Surely it is the right of all English people to hold their own opinions, and to shout them in the street if they choose? I am sad to think that King Henry, whose roar of laughter has gladdened the court as often as his rages have silenced it, has lost all humour. Our great, outrageous, theatrical monarch is turning before our eyes into a tight-mouthed tyrant.

25th March 1534

Under the new Act, all citizens have to swear an oath of allegiance to Henry as Supreme Head of the State and of the Church. Nobody in the court refused, naturally, though there are many who obeyed only out of fear. I count myself among these, but with my new baby due to be born any day now, how can I do otherwise? I have not been to Mass for a long time, but if God can really listen to an ordinary woman who speaks only for herself, I hope He will understand that I have to work in the Queen's service and also to care for my little boy and my husband. I get very tired sometimes. It is no excuse, I know, for neglecting my religion. I do think about it, but I am not the stuff of which martyrs are made.

There are some who are. Thomas Abell, who was for a long time Catherine's chaplain, has been accused of treason because he steadfastly refuses to take the oath. Both he and John Fisher, no longer recognized as a bishop, have been imprisoned in the Tower, pending trial.

I find myself full of despair tonight. We seem surrounded by cruelty, and my strength fails me.

1st April 1534

My feeling of sudden weakness gave way that same night to the first pains of birth. It was a long labour, but by four the next afternoon my little daughter was born. She is a fine, big child, and Tom adores her. I would have liked to call her Catherine, but it is too dangerous, so she is to be Maria, after the ex-Queen's close friend, Maria de Salinas.

It was a long and difficult birth, and for two days I was very ill, but my strength is starting to return now. William comes up from the kitchen as often as he can, bringing me bowls of soup and small slices of lean meat. He is such a kind boy.

11th April 1534

A letter came from Mama today, and I had to laugh when I heard her news. The Pope, years too late, has judged King Henry's new marriage to be illegal. He has commanded the King to take Catherine back, and to pay the whole costs of the case, which must by now be astronomical. His Holiness might as well try to put a thunderstorm into a cooking pot.

Tom tells me Sir Thomas More has for the second time refused to take the oath of allegiance. He resigned from office two years ago, and since then Henry has constantly tried to win his approval for the new religion, but with no success.

17th April 1534

Sir Thomas More was sent to the Tower today. He is imprisoned in the Bell Tower, just above the cell where John Fisher is still being held. So much for old friendship.

Henry and Anne have been to Eltham Palace to visit little Elizabeth and to inspect the nursery that is being prepared for "the coming prince", as they confidently call their expected baby. They seem to have great faith in the power of their own wishing. I suppose it is natural to them, when everything else they can dream of is theirs to command. But the womb is mysterious, and its workings are known only to the will of God.

20th April 1534

Today the Nun of Kent and four others convicted of high treason paid a dreadful price for their crimes. They were taken from their cells in the Tower to a gibbet, where they were hanged, but not mercifully. Before they were dead, they were cut down and then beheaded.

13th May 1534

The Queen's small household has now been sent to Kimbolton Castle in Huntingdonshire. The rider who came from there today says it is a pleasant place, but Catherine has been allocated only two rooms. To my great joy he brought letters from Mama and Rosanna. Rosanna says the Bishop of Durham came the other day and tried to make Catherine take the oath. He even reminded her of the death penalty for refusing, but although she is very ill now, with terrible pains in her chest, she continued to refuse.

The Queen taught her servants well. Those who claimed to speak no English were allowed to take the oath in Spanish, and they said, "*El Rey se ha heco cabeza de la Iglesia*," which means, "The King has made himself head of the Church," and is no oath at all. What spirit Catherine has!

28th June 1534

A disaster has occurred, but it is being hushed up. Anne has lost the baby she was expecting. Nobody knows if the child was still-born or died shortly after the birth. We do not even know whether it was a boy or a girl, if it was christened or where it is buried. I am haunted by the knowledge that this small soul was so unlovingly disposed of after its few minutes in this world.

The whole thing is a mystery. Anne was nearly eight months pregnant, so the baby should have had a good chance of survival. None of the ladies known to me attended the birth, only the King's physician. Anne is up and about again now, seeming no worse for the experience except that her face is white and anxious, but Henry is grim with disappointment. Certainly he is fast losing faith in the wife who has cost him so much trouble and made him so unpopular.

8th September 1534

A letter from Mama says Catherine's health is much worse now. She barely eats anything, and the constant pain makes it hard for her to sleep. I had suspected this to be true, for I heard that Lady Willoughby, once Maria de Salinas, after whom my little daughter is named, had begged the King for permission to visit her old friend. He would not allow it.

I was glad to remain behind when the court went on progress this summer. It has been good to have some time with Tom and Michael and baby Maria in peace, free of the tensions and rumours of court life. I have been busy, of course, helping with the big task of cleaning and refurbishing the castle here at Windsor, ready for another year's occupancy, but I am not troubled by that. Fresh whitewash and the smell of new rushes bring their own cheerfulness.

2nd October 1534

The court is back, buzzing and twittering like the swallows that gathered a week or two ago before they flew off in the other direction, away from the English winter. Anne Boleyn's elder sister Mary is here, pregnant by her new and undistinguished husband, William Stafford. She married him secretly, and her father is furious, but she seems very happy.

Pope Clement died on 26th September. The new Pope has not yet been elected, but whoever he is, I am sure he will be shocked by what is going on here. Pig-face Cromwell has started a tour of inspection of all the convents and monasteries, and is closing many of them, confiscating their wealth for the Crown.

The King approves of this. With the lavishness of his court life, I am sure he will find the money welcome.

8th October 1534

Anne's sister, Mary Boleyn, has been dismissed from the court. Her father so disapproved of her undistinguished second marriage that he cut off her allowance – and Anne then banished her. What kind of sisterly love is that? Mary did not seem concerned. I heard her say she would rather beg for bread with a good man at her side than be Queen of England. Rumour has it that she is going to put this in a letter to Pig-face! Anne is looking greatly annoyed, and I am sure someone has told her what her sister said.

17th October 1534

One of the grooms told Tom a dreadful story today. The King had been to see little Elizabeth, and when he was riding near Eltham Palace, he overtook a man called William Webb, who was riding a horse with his pretty sweetheart mounted behind him. Henry leaned across without a word to the man and dragged the girl over to his own saddle. Then he turned his horse and set off back to the Palace with her. This is not the first time he has done such a thing. These days he is indifferent to Anne's rages.

18th November 1534

Chabot de Brion, the Admiral of France, is here on a state visit. There is talk of a betrothal between little Elizabeth and one of the French king's sons, so there was a great banquet in the Admiral's honour. Anne sat beside her husband, richly dressed and trying her best to look sparkling and attractive. She has never been recognized as Henry's wife by the French, and she hopes through this engagement to be acknowledged as the rightful Queen of England. However, she looks much older now. Her pale face is beginning to set into bitter lines, and she seems scrawny rather than slim. Worst of all, she does not have the good sense to control her fury with Henry.

At one point during the ball that followed the feasting, the King went to fetch the Admiral's secretary from across the big room, and on his way paused to talk to a pretty woman. Anne saw this and burst into angry laughter. The Admiral thought she was laughing at him, and was about to take great offence, so she had to explain. "My husband went to fetch your secretary," she said, "but he met a lady who made him forget about it!" And she went into another peal of mirthless laughter. It was horribly embarrassing.

30th December 1534

This has been a difficult Christmas. It began with a shouting match between Anne and her own uncle, the Duke of Norfolk. This is not the first time they have quarrelled. I was not close enough to hear what Anne said, only that she was shouting at him in a temper – but I did hear the Duke call her dreadful names. He afterwards complained to Henry that Anne had used words to him "that should not be used to a dog", and the King was more than ready to believe him.

Anne speaks far more lovingly to her canine friends than she does to most human beings, including her husband, and there was a second Christmas calamity when her favourite dog died. She adored him and called him Little Purkoy, from the French word *"pourquoi"*, meaning "why", because he had such an enquiring expression. Nobody dared tell her he was dead, and eventually the King had to break the news himself. There was much weeping and lamentation.

Now that baby Maria is a little older, Madam Anne commands my presence as an entertainer again. I have been playing and singing all day today with the other musicians, trying to bring some joy to this tense and gloomy house. I urged Mark Smeaton to look merry as he played, but he is far too nervous of the royal moods to risk anything as rash as a smile. Anne used to flirt with him before she became so bitter, but he never seemed sure how to respond, having little wit and no lightness of touch. I have heard him boast that the Queen is secretly in love with him, but nobody takes that seriously. All musicians know their listeners sometimes fall in love with the music and think themselves in love with the player. Papa used to laugh about it. "A professional hazard," he used to say. But Mark, poor thing, has little sense of humour.

8th February 1535

Anne has suggested Madge Shelton as the King's new mistress! She cannot stop his philandering, so she is trying to have a controlling hand in it. We are all vastly amused. Madge, to my amazement, is delighted by the idea. Myself, I would hate to get mixed up in the dangerous politics of being a royal mistress – and besides, Henry is not what he was. He is putting on weight, and complains often of headaches. The old sore on his leg has developed into an abscess, and has to be bandaged all the time. I have helped change the dressings myself sometimes, and the smell of the open wound is very bad. The King is in constant pain with it, which does not improve his temper. But I suppose Madge will put up with such disadvantages for the sake of royal favours and presents.

19th February 1535

Madge goes about with a smug smile, and the King looks pleased with himself. Anne, on the other hand, seems more wretched every day. Her mouth is pinched in suspicious bitterness, and her dark eyes have lost their lustre, narrowed between puffy lids. It was a mistake to choose a lady so well known to us as her husband's mistress – it has made her a laughing stock.

17th March 1535

Anne finds she is pregnant again, so she looks more cheerful. The King is paying more attention to her since she announced this news, and his interest in Madge Shelton seems to be waning.

7th May 1535

Three days ago, the Prior of Charterhouse Monastery was hanged, drawn and quartered, and so were four monks of the same Carthusian order. They paid the penalty for refusing to take the oath of allegiance to Henry's new Church. I feel cold and sickened at the thought of it.

In spite of the executions, John Fisher has again refused to take the King's oath, and so has Sir Thomas More. The two of them are still in the Tower. Anne

Boleyn is urging the King to put them to death, but both these men are old and trusted friends. Mama told me once that Thomas More used to take Henry up to the roof of Greenwich Palace when he was a boy, to look at the stars. The pair of them shared a passion for astronomy, and More taught young Henry all he knew about the heavenly bodies. Surely the King must remember that? But it seems that Henry has no cares now for old memories or human decencies. He will condemn his old friend for the sake of his new religion. I pray for Thomas More, and admire his courage in holding to the true faith.

Anne is trying hard to improve her popularity with the people. She gives money to the poor, and when she visits a town or village, she sends her stewards ahead to find out if there are widows or destitute people in special need of help. She has provided for the education of several impoverished students at Cambridge – but when it comes to enforcing the new religion, she urges the King on in his cruelties.

22nd June 1535

John Fisher was beheaded at the Tower this morning. He was 76 years old. I wish Henry could have allowed him the dignity of a natural death in the fullness of time.

More Carthusian monks have been executed. This time the men were chained upright to stakes and left there to die slowly, in the humiliation of their own excrement. Londoners are not easily shocked – they watch executions as though they were fairground amusements, and walk past the rotting heads of traitors impaled on London Bridge with no more than an occasional complaint about the smell – but they found the deliberate brutality of these deaths appalling.

29th June 1535

Anne has for a second time lost her expected baby. It had seemed a healthy pregnancy, and at six months she was a good size with the child, so the cause is a mystery. Henry has little sympathy for her shock and grief. He is now blaming her for the executions that are making him so unpopular in the country, saying she forced him into them. Some whisper that he has begun to think Anne is a witch, and has put a spell on him to make him love her.

When love ends, does not everyone feel that a spell is broken? I cannot imagine ceasing to love Tom, but in moments when we have had some silly argument, I have felt bereft of love, and that is bad enough.

As to the question of witchcraft – how many women have been condemned by such a convenient accusation? It takes only the smallest abnormality or the slightest sign of being too clever, and tongues begin to wag about supernatural powers. It is very easy for Henry to call Anne a witch. She has a fingernail that sprouts beside the normal one on the little finger of her left hand, and they say there are warts on her body that could be the sign of the Devil. But the King did not object to these things in all the years he has declared Anne to be the love of his life, and he will need a better reason than that if he is to get rid of her.

6th July 1535

After a five-day-long trial, Sir Thomas More, the King's boyhood friend and lifetime adviser, was found guilty of high treason. He was beheaded on Tower Hill today. No words can express my horror and sadness.

11th July 1535

William Somers, the jester who took over when Papa died, went too far this evening. In a merry bit of fooling, he made some cheeky remarks about Anne and called the infant Elizabeth "a bastard". I was not present, so have no idea what he thought he was up to, but the results were instant. Henry has banned him from the court.

William is lucky. Until recently, such a dangerous joke could have cost him his life. Things have changed now, and the jester's instinct was right. Henry is no longer seriously angry with those who mock his wife. I suspect he is secretly pleased.

15th July 1535

The King of France has agreed that his third son may be betrothed to little Elizabeth, who is not yet two years old. Anne is delighted, and Henry seems pleased as well. The one thing the royal pair still have in common is their love for their red-haired baby, and they often go to see her at Hatfield or Eltham.

The summer progress starts soon, and this year I have to go with the court. Tom will be there as well, and we can take Michael and the baby with us, so I am quite looking forward to it. Little Maria is fifteen months old now, and is almost weaned, and there will be plenty of other people to look after her if I have to be with the Queen. We are to go first to Winchcombe, then to various places in Wales, and back through the county of Wiltshire.

29th October 1535

The King has fallen in love with yet another serving lady. This time it is Jane Seymour, who was in Catherine's service with me. She left when the Queen was sent away to The More. I remember her telling me at the time that she was fond of Catherine, but she thought it more sensible to stay in the King's court. Jane has always been very sensible. She is rather plain and has no sparkle at all, which is probably why Henry likes her. She is as different from Anne as any woman could be.

We stayed at Wulfhall during the summer travels, the house of Sir John Seymour, Jane's father. He does not sparkle, either. He is sheriff of Wiltshire, Dorset and Somerset, and owns a lot of land, but he is no aristocrat, merely a wealthy farmer. He was greatly excited to have the King of England under his roof, and could not do enough to make us all comfortable.

There is a great scandal about Sir John. For years he conducted an affair with the wife of his own son, and they say he fathered her two children.

His son found out, of course, and there was fearful trouble. For a long time the family was split by deep hatreds, but we saw no sign of that during our time at Wulfhall.

Since our return the King has been paying Jane Seymour a lot of attention, and most people assume she will soon become his new mistress. I am not so sure. Jane lowers her eyes modestly at Henry's advances. She seems quite incapable of flirting, and just looks very sensible and very good. This may be due to the advice of her brothers, Thomas and Edward, who are both at court. They know perfectly well that Anne Boleyn became Queen by remaining virtuous, and clearly hope their sister can do the same thing. I groan at the thought. Do we have to go through another tedious and troublesome royal divorce? Life at this court is constantly packed with drama, and there are times when I long for simple peace.

30th October 1535

The harvest has been very bad this year, and people are blaming it on Anne. They are sure that God is angry with their king for putting away his rightful wife, and fear that they are being forced to share his punishment.

Anne keeps urging Henry to "get rid" of Catherine. It is as if she cannot believe herself to be the true queen while Catherine of Aragon lives and enjoys the support of the people. I am sure Henry would like to see his ex-wife dead, but for very different reasons. He cannot think of marrying Jane Seymour with two previous wives still living. Even with all his powers, the complications of such a move are too awful to think of. But it would suit him nicely if both Catherine *and* Anne were to die. Perhaps Anne has not thought of that. Meanwhile, she has no hope of persuading Henry to bring about the old Queen's death. The people would rise against him in rebellion, and the Emperor Charles would be his sworn enemy. Our king is too wise a statesman to risk these things.

6th November 1535

The King's problem may be solved by natural means
before very long. Mama's last letter tells me Catherine
is desperately ill, barely able to breathe for the terrible
pains in her chest. Mama is sure it is partly brought on
by worry. Catherine has not enough money to pay the
few servants left to her, and she frets about it
continually. Weak as she is, last week she struggled to
sit up and write to her nephew, the Emperor, begging
him to send her some money. I doubt whether he will
take any notice, as he is busy fighting the Turks. It
grieves me that this great lady should come to the end
of her life in this pathetic way, no more noticed than a
beggar in a gutter.

12th November 1535

Anne let it be known today that she is pregnant again. The King is pleased, but not ecstatic. After two failures, he probably doubts whether she will ever give him another living child. We can all see he has lost interest in her. His eyes turn constantly to Jane, the modest little dormouse who might – who knows? – be good at having babies.

16th December 1535

This is Queen Catherine's 50th birthday. I still call her Queen, if only in the privacy of my diary, for it is the only respect I can pay her. How extraordinary it is that a queen of England should achieve half a century of royal life, first as a Spanish princess then as Queen of England, without a flag waved or a trumpet blown.

A letter came from Rosanna today with the good news that she is expecting another baby. It will be born next summer, in early July, she thinks.

She said that the Queen managed to leave her bed for a few hours the other day, and sit on a chair. Evidently Anne has been told the same thing, for she flew into a panic of rage and alarm at the thought that her hated rival might recover. She ran to the King, demanding to know why he could not bring about the woman's death, and threatening that she herself would kill Catherine, and Mary as well, if he had no stomach for it. Henry's face was stony. He has no sympathy, either for his first wife or his present one.

27th December 1535

Somehow we got through another Christmas, though there was little joy in it. The Spanish ambassador, Chapuys, who is deeply grieved by Catherine's plight, sat unsmiling through the celebrations, and the whole court is uneasy. Jane's relatives fawn upon the King, while the Boleyn supporters become daily more strident, quarrelling among themselves and blaming Anne for letting them down. They are such unpleasant people.

29th December 1535

Chapuys has had a letter from Catherine's physicians, asking urgently that he should come to see her before it is too late. It is whispered that the doctors fear she is being poisoned, and do not want to be left to decide on their own whether this is happening.

Chapuys went to see the King, and came out grim-faced, though with permission to make the journey. Henry had expressed no regrets about Catherine. He merely remarked that once she was dead, the Emperor would have no more reason to act against him. Chapuys rode off to Kimbolton an hour later. Pray God he may be in time.

8th January 1536

Catherine of Aragon died yesterday at two in the afternoon. The messenger who brought the news gave me a letter from Mama that was smudged with her tears. On the previous day she and the other ladies had helped the Queen to sit up because she wanted to write to Henry. She could hardly hold the pen, but she wrote of her love for him, and of her innocence. She said she forgave him everything, and prayed that God would do likewise. She bade him be a good father to Mary. And as a last gesture of defiance, she signed herself "Catherine the Queen".

The messenger told us Maria de Salinas forced her way past the guards, who had orders not to let her in. I am so glad of that. At least Catherine had her old friend with her when she died.

An autopsy was carried out last night, before Catherine's body was sealed in a lead casket, and a black growth was found on her heart. Her doctors are sure it is a sign of poison, and those who cared for her said she seemed much worse after drinking some Welsh-brewed beer. We will never know the truth – but thousands of people in England will be convinced that Anne Boleyn is a murderess, and perhaps not for the first time.

10th January 1536

Last night a magnificent ball was held. I found it distasteful, with Catherine not yet buried, but the King had no such scruples. When told of his first wife's death, he seemed merely relieved. Anne of course was delighted. She said, "Now I am truly a queen!"

The royal couple wore yellow at the ball, because that is the colour of mourning in Spain. Henry has ordered a fine funeral to be laid on in Peterborough, where Catherine is to be buried on the 29th of this month. Anne seemed happy, naturally enough, and the King paraded little Elizabeth before the assembled company, as if to underline that she would be the future Queen of England. Princess Mary should inherit the crown, being the elder of the royal daughters, but she will be ignored.

This morning Anne's gaiety had evaporated. She sent for me to play, but when I went in with my lute she was sitting by the window, weeping. I asked if there was anything I could do for her, but she shook her head. I began to play a quiet pavane, and after a while she dried her eyes. When the tune ended she said, "You are a lucky girl, Ellie. You have so much. A good husband. Music at your fingertips. Children." Her lips quivered again, and she looked away out of the window with its diamond panes. They were coated with frost, for the newly lit fire had not yet started to warm the room.

I began to play again, a galliard this time, hoping the faster pace would cheer her, and eventually she put away her handkerchief, but her face remained anxious and unsmiling.

I know the cause of her distress. If the child she is carrying should fail to live Henry will discard her, just as he discarded his first wife. Anne thought she would be secure once Catherine was dead, but in fact it is the other way round. Now the old queen has gone, Henry has only one wife to deal with – and Anne has none of Catherine's influence with the people or with the powerful families of Europe. She is more vulnerable now than she has ever been. Staring out of those frosted windows, she stared at a terrible truth that she can no longer fend off. She, like Catherine, may end her life alone and ignored. Her dream of glittering triumph as the Queen of England is turning to ashes.

12th January 1536

Catherine's household is to be disbanded. Henry sent men to collect all her possessions, apparently to help pay for her funeral expenses. Mama was much grieved. She did not mind so much about the valuable things, like the little clock set in a jewelled golden book or the double portrait of Henry and Catherine, but the small things upset her. "Why did he have to take her nightgowns and her slippers?" her letter demanded, "and even the little clothes she had set by for each of her hoped-for babies?"

There are other things to worry about, more closely touching our family. The King is sending all Catherine's Spanish servants back to Spain. Mama is distressed about this. She is 50 years old, and says she cannot go back now to a country she left when she was sixteen. Everything that matters to her is in England. My brothers are working here at Henry's court, so they will stay. Tom and I are here, and Michael and Maria. "I will never see them again," her letter lamented. "I will miss all their growing up."

Rosanna will go with her husband. Diego was born here, it is true, but he has always wanted to go back to Granada, where his parents come from. They themselves returned there some years ago, when Catherine moved into The More with her reduced staff, and they write often to Diego. He is full of longing to see all the things they describe – the Moorish tiles, the fountains, the oranges hanging on trees in the sunshine. Rosanna is excited at the idea, too. Little John will love it, she said, and how wonderful for the new baby to be born in a place of sunshine and warmth!

Mama must come and live with us, of course. I know she will never consent to serve Anne Boleyn, but perhaps there is some work she can do in the court. If nothing else, she is a wonderfully fine embroideress. Chapuys says he will ask Jane Seymour to have a word with the King about it.

24th January 1536

While jousting today, Henry collided with another rider and both he and his horse crashed to the ground. The King was unconscious for two hours, and there was panic that he might die. When the Duke of Norfolk told Anne what had happened she remained remarkably calm, but I wondered as I looked at her whether she was simply too shocked to speak.

This evening Dr Butts said the King was out of danger, but he is still far from well. The old injury to his leg is badly infected and steadily worsening, and he is in great pain despite our constant bandaging. He should not have been jousting, of course. He is heavy and paunchy now, and he has lost much of his athletic prowess, though he will never admit it. His good looks are fading, too. The flesh on his face has thickened, making his eyes look smaller, and his mouth is tight and bad-tempered. The red-gold hair that was such a glory has receded, and he is almost completely bald. At 46, he still thinks himself young and attractive, but it is getting harder for the rest of us to see him that way.

28th January 1536

Mama arrived this evening with a small trunk containing her few possessions. Diego and Rosanna are here, too. John is three now, a bundle of black-haired energy. They will set out for Dover next week to take ship for Spain. I can hardly bear to think about it. Tom tried to cheer me up, saying we will go to see them one day when the children are older. Perhaps we will. After all, Papa moved about all over Europe, earning a living through his playing and fooling, and I am his daughter. A long journey should mean nothing to me. But for now, there are practical things to be done.

Mama looks thin and tired, and her clothes are in a terrible state, shabby and much-darned. I will lend her a gown of mine until I can get some fabric to make a new one. It may be that Anne will let me have some since she has more silk and velvet and brocade than she can possibly use.

30th January 1536

Yesterday was Queen Catherine's funeral. The King did not go to Peterborough for it, and neither, needless to say, did Anne. In the morning a solemn Mass was held in the chapel here at Greenwich, and I was glad to see that Henry was in black. Anne wore yellow, and grumbled that such a fuss was being made.

That was only the beginning of a disastrous day. Later in the afternoon Anne came into a room and found Jane Seymour sitting on Henry's knee, and flew into a terrible rage. She slammed off into her own quarters, and stayed there. I was not serving her. Madge had kindly said she would take my place so that I could look after Mama, who has a bad cold after the journey, and so I only learned this morning what had happened.

Anne had a miscarriage in the night. They say the child would have been a boy. It is the worst of tragedies for her. Madge said the King walked into her bedchamber where she lay sobbing and uttered no word of sympathy. Instead, he berated her for the loss of "his boy". Anne, of course, shouted back at him, even in her distress. It was his own fault, she said, for flaunting his liking for "that wench, Jane Seymour". Henry stormed out, saying she should have no more children by him.

Anne is trying to put a bright face on it today. Now that Catherine is dead, she says, there will be no more malign influence at work, and her next child will live. We were careful not to look at each other, but the same thought was in all our minds. There will be no next child. Anne Boleyn has had her last chance.

26th February 1536

Diego and Rosanna left last week. I managed not to weep, knowing it would make the parting worse. Tom reminds me that I saw very little of them when they were in Queen Catherine's service. "Away is away," he said. "It makes no difference whether they are in Spain or Kimbolton." He is right, of course. It's just that Spain somehow *feels* further.

The King left Greenwich a few days ago to attend the Shrovetide celebrations in London. He did not take Anne. Last week he sent Sir Nicholas Carew with a love letter and presents for Jane Seymour, but there were none for his wife, who is very cast down by this. She takes it as a sign that her husband truly means to divorce her. I am afraid she is right.

Among Jane's gifts there was a purse of gold, together with a letter. We all watched to see whether she would accept Henry's money – but she did not. She kissed the unopened letter with great respect then handed it back to Sir Nicholas, together with the purse. She fell on her knees and humbly bade him tell the King she was a chaste and virtuous woman. If His Majesty wished to send her money, she said, she prayed him to do so as an engagement gift when she had "a husband to marry". Her modesty is impeccable, but her intention is plain. She will settle for nothing less than marriage.

Meanwhile, she remains in Anne's service, and the Queen stares at her with bitter enmity. She would like to dismiss her, but she dares not.

1st March 1536

Anne gave me some heavy silk to make a gown for Mama. Even better, she agreed without any argument to let her work as a needlewoman, making and embroidering clothes for little Elizabeth, who is fast growing out of her dresses. Mama wanted to refuse when I told her of the offer, saying she would not work for "that woman". I was a little sharp with her, and pointed out that Queen Catherine is dead now. There is no point in continuing a fight that is ended – and the old queen would not have wanted to see her old and faithful friend cast into penury. Mama gave in, but she says she will only work for the little princess, not for Anne herself.

5th March 1536

Henry is back here at Greenwich. As soon as he returned, he told Cromwell to move out of his rooms adjacent to the King's own quarters, and gave Jane the use of them instead. He installed Jane's brother and his wife in the same suite, to act as chaperones, but it is rumoured that a door from Jane's room connects via a gallery to his own.

Anne is hysterical with fury. She slapped Jane's face yesterday, not for the first time. She has the right to chastise her servants, but this was sheer jealousy. Jane seems unperturbed. This morning, she was provocatively opening and shutting a locket containing Henry's miniature, and Anne snatched it from her neck so roughly that she cut the side of her own hand on its gold chain. I had to bandage it for her. She was weeping as I did so, and she leaned her head towards me a little, as if she would have liked an arm round her shoulders in comfort. I almost responded, for I know she is in great distress, but she is not a child like Michael or Maria, she is the Queen of England. So I curtsied and moved away.

2nd April 1536

Anne has had me with her every day in the past weeks, bidding me sing and play and make her laugh, but it is increasingly hard to keep up my own spirits. This queen has been cruel and self-seeking, I admit, but she is being discarded because she bore three dead children, which seems very harsh. I remember the words Queen Catherine spoke to me – "Every woman carries grief." Anne Boleyn knows that now.

7th April 1536

Jane Seymour has left Greenwich in the company of her brother Edward and his wife. They are going home to Wulfhall, though nobody knows why. Jane has been saying she is weary of the lewd jokes at her expense that fly round the court, but we all think there is more to it than that. I remember how Henry sent Anne away to Hever when his case against Catherine was being heard, and wonder if he has some plan afoot. He spends long hours closeted with Cromwell these days, and I am sure they are plotting something.

The King is to dissolve Parliament next week, on 14th April. This is much earlier than usual. Tom says it can only be to make sure the Queen does not appeal to its justice if Henry seeks to divorce her.

23rd April 1536

Cromwell has been away from court for the whole week. He came back this morning, and went straight to see King Henry. Various courtiers paused outside the closed door, ostensibly to brush a crumb from a sleeve or do up a lace, but their listening brought them no hint of what the murmuring voices were saying. Rumours and speculation are rife, of course, but nobody knows what the King and his closest adviser are up to.

24th April 1536

Cromwell has been questioning all of us who serve the Queen, asking if we know if any men have visited Anne in her private rooms. I said with truth that I did not, but he went on pressing me. One of Anne's maids had reported several names, he said. I doubted this so much that I asked him who they were, and his answer made me gasp. He listed Sir Henry Norris, Sir Francis Weston and Anne's own brother, Rochford. Then he added a fourth man, William Brereton, and lastly he mentioned Mark Smeaton.

It was so absurd that I hardly knew what to say. Henry Norris has been close to the King for years, and he is the kindest and most courteous of men. I remember how he offered Wolsey his own room on that dreadful occasion when the Cardinal was left standing in the courtyard with no provision made for him – and it was he who relieved Henry of his squawking peacock and pelican not so long ago. Sir Francis Weston has no eyes for anyone but his young wife and his baby son, and I told Cromwell this. He asked if I knew William

Brereton, but I did not. Then he said I could hardly deny that I knew Mark Smeaton.

I told him Mark was innocent, but he was not satisfied. He observed that Mark has a romantic manner of speaking and behaving. This is true, of course, but I explained that many musicians get into this habit, because people sigh over the sweetness of the lute songs and expect the singer to be as romantic as the music. I did not tell Cromwell what everyone knows, that the Queen often flirted with Mark as she flirted with many of the court gentlemen. All of us who entertain kings and queens accept that we have to wear a face of bright gaiety when a royal person is in flirtatious mood, even if we are tired or hungry or longing to lie down and nurse a headache. Mark, as a court musician, has to entertain the Queen and amuse her, but it means no more than that. I told Cromwell this last bit, because it seemed safe as well as true, and his small eyes kept a cold watch on me as I spoke. Then he said, "So Master Smeaton would do anything his mistress commanded." It was a twisting of my words, and I frowned. "We all do what the King and Queen command," I said. His lips tightened into something that was not quite a smile, and he wrote a note on the paper he held. I wish I knew what it was.

28th April 1536

There are rumours that the Privy Council is considering the matter of a royal divorce. Someone asked the Bishop of London whether Henry meant to abandon his wife, but the Bishop refused to reply.

I wonder if Anne secretly fears something worse. Two days ago she asked her chaplain, Matthew Parker, to be responsible for little Elizabeth if the child should be left motherless. I saw Parker as he came out of the chapel, and he looked shocked. I didn't know at the time what Anne had said to him, but it leaked out, as all secrets do in this court. I understand now why the chaplain was appalled, for the same horror and disbelief laid cold fingers on me as well. King Henry may be planning not merely to divorce Anne but to bring about her execution. The idea has run round like wildfire, and everyone is whispering in corners.

The King, of course, shows no sign of thinking any such thing. He plans to go to Dover in a week's time, to inspect the new fortifications there, and as far as we know, he still intends to take Anne with him. Tom will be with the party as well, in case of any mishap with the horses on the way. I will not be needed, but I am in the usual turmoil of packing and preparation, with Anne constantly changing her mind about which dresses to take and which jewellery to wear. We are all wondering now if this journey will really happen, or whether it is an elaborate pretence. Henry has always been a good actor, and at the moment he is all innocence. But a cat that has stolen the cream can also look innocent.

29th April 1536

The King met with Cromwell and all his advisers this morning. There was the usual drone of voices through the closed doors – and then we heard Henry shouting in absolute outrage. "I knew it! I always suspected it!" When he came out, his face was livid with anger and he stormed off to his own quarters without speaking to anyone. Is this acting, too, or is it genuine? Nobody can guess.

Cromwell looks pleased with himself, and all the men who had been at the meeting have an air of new and important resolution. But they are saying nothing.

30th April 1536

Anne walked her dogs in Greenwich Park this morning as usual, and I was with her, together with several of her other ladies. When we returned, we found a crowd of people assembled outside the palace. I asked a man what was happening, and he said an important meeting was going on and they were all waiting to hear what was decided. He glanced at Anne as he spoke, then quickly looked away.

The Queen did not say anything. She went straight to the nursery and gathered up her small daughter, who is here at present, then carried her out to stand in the courtyard below the King's window. She told all of us to leave her, but I watched from a distance and saw her gestures of entreaty as she looked up at her husband. I could not hear what either of them said.

I came up here for a moment of solitude, and to write down this strange event. I have a terrible feeling of foreboding.

Midnight, the same day

Mark Smeaton was arrested later this morning. They accused him of having adulterous relations with the Queen, and took him to Cromwell's house in Stepney for questioning.

I keep asking myself whether Mark could possibly be guilty. He played for the Queen in her outer room occasionally, and I once saw him give a sly wink to a friend, saying Anne was wonderful in bed, but I just assumed he was joking. Anne Boleyn would never look at a mere lute player with a skinny body and lank hair. Or would she? If he caught her at a moment when she was feeling bereft and lonely, it could have been possible, I suppose. Poor Mark will never have the courage to deny it, because he always agrees with whatever his superiors say. So far this has kept him in favour, but it will do him no good now. He must defend himself, and vigorously.

Again and again I wonder if what I told Cromwell has counted against him. "We all do what the King and Queen command." It was no more than the truth, and I meant only to affirm Mark's innocence. Did Pig-face interpret it as a tacit confirmation of his guilt? I cannot bear the thought.

Nobody knows yet what it was that so angered the King at yesterday's meeting, but the planned visit to Dover has been abandoned. They were to depart in two days' time, so to cancel it at such short notice must mean something important is afoot. Everyone says it is to do with Mark's arrest. If he is found guilty, then Anne will be found guilty too – for it takes two to commit adultery. I cannot help wondering if the whole thing is a trap set by Henry and Cromwell to ensnare the Queen.

Madge says that even if Anne has been unfaithful, it does not count as treason against the King, but if she and her lover are suspected of plotting Henry's overthrow, it does. And the penalty for treason is death.

Henry was stalking about with an injured expression today, as if hurt and astonished that his wife has made him a cuckold. This time I am sure he is play-acting. If he and Pig-face have devised this plot against Anne, then he is obviously not astonished at all. Yes, I think he planned it himself, and behind the pretended innocence there is a cold determination to rid himself of his wife, no matter if it costs her life and Mark's. The King has become a monster.

Oh, what a risk I take in writing such words! I hide this diary carefully, and pray that nobody finds it – but to write the truth, even secretly, is a small relief to me in the nightmare that is closing round us. I am beginning to hate this court. I wish Tom and I could be far away with our children, living as ordinary people do, knowing no more of these cruel storms than they do of God's thunder that sometimes shakes the sky.

1st May 1536

On this May Day a great tournament went ahead as though everything was normal. Anne sat beside the King on the royal dais, watching the proceedings. She seemed unaware that Mark was no longer at court. I suppose nobody told her of his arrest.

Henry seemed particularly irritable, but we assumed it was because he could not take part in the jousting. After the accident in January his physicians have forbidden him to take any further risks, and he hates being a mere spectator. Normally he would have led one of the sides in their mock war, but today their leaders were Sir Henry Norris and Anne's brother, Viscount Rochford. I could not help remembering that Pig-face had mentioned both men when questioning us about the Queen.

Halfway though the afternoon, the King got up abruptly and left the royal stand. Anne continued to sit there alone, but she looked puzzled and uneasy.

When the last event was over, the King rode into the arena. Ignoring everyone else, he brought his horse alongside that of Sir Henry Norris and escorted him out – but not, I thought, in friendship. Henry was grim-faced, and Norris seemed mildly surprised, though he greeted the King with his usual affable courtesy. The two of them went off together.

2nd May 1536

This has been a terrible day.

Sir Henry Norris was arrested this morning, and sent to the Tower. He is accused of having criminal intercourse with the Queen. Apparently King Henry questioned him closely on their ride from the tournament yesterday, and was not satisfied with Norris's protestations of innocence. Even more grotesquely, Rochford was arrested on the same charge, though in his case it is also incest, for the Queen is his sister. They say Rochford's wife, who is a spiteful woman and on bad terms with her husband, gave evidence against him because she has always been jealous of his affection for Anne.

The Queen was watching a tennis match at the time of the arrests and suspected nothing. She was smiling, and I heard her say to Madge that she wished she had laid a bet on her favoured player, as he was winning so handsomely. Then a messenger came, and announced that Her Majesty was required to present herself at once to the gentlemen of the Privy Council. Anne sighed at having to miss the rest of the game, but she got up obediently and went to the council chamber.

I was one of the ladies who went with her, so I saw what happened. Anne's uncle, the Duke of Norfolk, was waiting for her at the door, and ushered her in. The assembled gentlemen then told the Queen she was accused of having committed adultery with Mark Smeaton, Sir Henry Norris and one other, whom they did not name. They added that the three men had confessed their guilt.

Anne did not weep or protest. She seemed stunned, as if she did not quite understand what had been said to her. We were told to escort her back to her chambers. An armed man came with us, and when we had gone in, he stationed himself outside the door, on guard.

Anne seemed indignant rather than afraid. She was desperately concerned for the accused men, knowing they face the death sentence if adultery should be proved against them. Strangely, she did not seem to realize her own danger. Perhaps she thought the accusation too ridiculous to take seriously. After all, everyone in the court indulges in a little flirtation from time to time – it means nothing. Or perhaps it was like her worst nightmare come true, and she could not believe she was not asleep and dreaming.

Some of Anne's ladies are secret supporters of Jane Seymour, and they glanced at each other with small, malicious smiles. Anne was careful not to look at them. The rest of us did our best to reassure her. I have had no cause ever to like Anne Boleyn, but my heart went out to her today, and I gave her what comfort I could. Anne seemed to believe that everything could be explained and smoothed over, and recovered something of her old spirit. We accompanied her to the dining chamber, escorted by the man stationed as a guard, and she set about her food with normal appetite.

She was still at the table when the door was flung open. The Duke of Norfolk came in, together with Cromwell and several other courtiers. Anne rose and asked their business, and her uncle unrolled a parchment he carried. He told her it was a warrant for her arrest. She was to go to the Tower, and remain there "to abide during His Highness's pleasure".

I thought it astonishing that Anne remained so calm. Her voice was quite steady as she answered. "If it be His Majesty's pleasure, I am ready to obey," she said. And they took her away. We were not even allowed to pack some clothes for her.

The net continues to close. Riders have been sent to arrest William Brereton, whom I have never met, and Sir Francis Weston. He lives at Sutton Place in Surrey, with his wife and baby son. He used to play tennis with the King. *Used to*. I am already writing of him as though his life was past. I feel sick to my soul at what is happening.

Jane Seymour's supporters are openly gloating now. How quickly everything has changed! Until a few months ago, every English citizen was being forced to swear allegiance to Anne Boleyn, and people were executed for refusing. Among ourselves, it was dangerous to express anything but the warmest liking for the Queen. And now she is suddenly the witch who enchanted the King then betrayed him, a wicked woman who plotted his downfall while sleeping with his enemies.

Tom and I walked down the grassy hill here at Greenwich to the river this evening, enjoying the fading daylight. Now that Mama is here we get away by ourselves more often, as she loves to be with the children. We met Will Cook, one of the Queen's bargemen, and he told us what happened this afternoon. Anne was escorted aboard at five o'clock, in full view of a great crowd of people standing round and gawping. Will was angry about that. Prisoners for the Tower are usually ferried there at night, he said, in the privacy of darkness, so why should she be denied this small mercy? Will has always shared the common view that this queen is a jumped-up harlot, but he was touched by Anne's plight today.

"That uncle of hers," he said. "For twopence I'd have tipped him in the river. Every minute of the way, he kept telling her the men accused have admitted their guilt. He seemed to glory in it. The lady never answered. Kept her mouth closed, stared anywhere but at him."

She collapsed when they reached the watergate at the Tower, though. All the strength had gone out of her, Will said, and he and the other men had to help her up the steps to where the Constable of the Tower stood waiting with his men. She sank on her knees, praying for God's help and swearing she was not guilty. She was weeping, and she asked, "Mr Kingston, do I go into a dungeon?"

Sir William Kingston is the Constable. He assured Anne she would be housed in the quarters she and Henry had occupied on the night before her coronation. She said, "It is too good for me," and burst into hysterical laughter mingled with tears. It must have been terrible for her, remembering that glorious day a scant three years ago, when the river was all aflutter with crimson and gold, and music rang out across the water. It must have been a bitter contrast with the darkness that faces her now.

Will said she managed to calm herself a little, and then she said, "May God bear witness there is no truth in these charges. I am as clear from the company of man as from sin." I am sure she speaks the truth. She has been guilty of her own cruelties, but she is not stupid. She would never have done anything which so obviously would lead to her downfall.

It grieves me that the ladies serving Anne in the Tower are not her friends. One of them is the Constable's wife, Lady Kingston, and there are two of her aunts who have never liked her. The fourth is a Mrs Cosyn, who is the wife of Anne's Master of Horse. They have been picked, I suspect, to watch the Queen rather than to serve her, and to report on any admission of her guilt. There is also Margaret Wyatt, sister to the poet who once loved Anne. Perhaps her only true friend among them is old Mrs Orchard, who was her childhood nurse. I am glad she is there.

3rd May 1536

Henry Fitzroy, the King's son by Bessie Blount, was at supper with his father this evening. When he stood up to say goodnight, the King took the young man in his arms, with tears in his eyes. He thanked God that young Henry and his half-sister, Mary, had escaped death at the hands of "that cursed and venomous whore, who tried to poison you both". He spoke as if he really believed his own words.

Young Henry does not look well. He has a constant cough, and sometimes lays his arm across his chest as if there is a pain in there. I think he has consumption. They can hardly blame Anne Boleyn for that.

7th May 1536

Yesterday we moved from Greenwich to Hampton Court. This will be more convenient for the King to visit Jane, who is now installed at Beddington Park, in Surrey. His Majesty is growing his beard again. Anne preferred him clean-shaven, but it is Jane Seymour's wishes that count now. Ever since Anne was imprisoned, Henry has been in a mood of wild celebration. He runs from one party to another, celebrating and carousing. But no doubt he finds time for Jane.

12th May 1536

Today has been dreadful. I had to go to Westminster Hall as a witness in the trial of poor Mark Smeaton, together with Norris, Brereton and Weston. The case against Anne and her brother will be heard after the weekend, at the Tower. We left Hampton Court early to get to Westminster, and the accused men were brought from the Tower by river.

Mark looked gaunt and thin, drained of all hope. It is whispered that he was put on the rack at the Tower, and tortured until he confessed. I hope that is not true. Mark would probably confess of his own accord, and I thank God for it. He is not a hero by nature – and what would be the point in incurring further suffering? Protestations of innocence would be useless. The grand plan does not allow for them. Mark has to be guilty.

I said I knew of no misconduct by any of the accused men. I was careful about my words, lest they be misused, and was quickly dismissed as being of no interest. Some of the ladies gave the court far more pleasure, retailing salacious stories of the Queen's promiscuity. Nobody queried the tales they told, even though some of the alleged offences were remembered – or misremembered – from years ago.

We all knew the men would be found guilty, but the manner of their execution is the barbaric one reserved for those committing high treason. Mark and the other three will be hanged, cut down while still alive, castrated and disembowelled. Their bodies will then be cut into quarters. Dear God, grant them a speedy escape of the spirit from such agony. May they rest in peace.

13th May 1536

The King commanded today that Anne's household at Greenwich is to be broken up and dispersed. Those of us who served her are all dismissed.

I do not know what Tom and I will do. Will the King want me to serve Jane Seymour? It is plain that he means to marry her as soon as Anne is out of the way. After little more than a week, he is tired of riding out from Hampton Court to see Jane in the Surrey house. He is removing himself to Whitehall tomorrow, and Jane is to take up residence at a house in the Strand, just a short walk away.

This may be the right time to leave the court and all its intrigues. I suspect that I am pregnant again, and I am in no mood to attend to the whims of yet another royal mistress. Jane Seymour irritates me in a way that Anne, for all her malevolence, never did. Jane has large, rather stupid eyes and a little mouth set above a weak chin. She looks as humble and stupid as a sheep. I suppose that is what the King likes about her. She has a certain obstinacy about getting her own way, but she always appears utterly meek. She is poorly educated and has not the wit to argue with anyone, let alone Henry. He will have no trouble in getting total obedience from Jane. But I find her just plain boring.

Tom and I have dreamed for years of a small place where we can live peacefully with our children, but the dream seems difficult and almost frightening now that we must think about turning it into reality. My brothers have been told they can go on working at Henry's court. William is pleased, for he likes his work in the kitchen. He helps with the cooking now, and especially loves preparing the spiced cakes and sugared fruits that look so delectable at banquets. He is neat-fingered and quick, and he is happy in the heat and the smell of spices and roasting meat. Daniel is different. He is impatient with the court, too blunt by nature to make a success of working there. He wants to come with us, and I am glad of it. He will be useful, helping Tom in the forge and with the field-work.

Mama does not say much. I wonder if she is secretly a little dismayed by our plans to abandon court life.

She has lived in the abundance – and sometimes the meanness – of royal households all her life, and leaving it perhaps frightens her a little. But there is nothing for her in Henry's court now. She has never forgiven the King for his treatment of Catherine, and although she has no sympathy for his new wife, Anne's fate confirms Mama's conviction that Henry has lost all humanity.

I am not sure she is right about this. It seems to me that the King is all too human when it comes to his own feelings. The trouble is, he fails to see that other people share the same worries and pains as he does. But at any rate, Mama says she would not stay even if Henry asked her. I am glad of this, for I would not like her to be regretting a lost way of life. She has had a hard time in these last years, and I think she will be happy with us once she gets used to the big change that has to happen. She loves the children, and they adore her. We must look for a place that has a good piece of land, then we can graze a cow and keep a pig and some chickens, and grow vegetables. Tom's trade as a blacksmith will bring in enough money for our other needs, especially with Daniel helping. But nothing can be done until the last scene of poor Anne's life has been played out.

15th May 1536

I went to the Great Hall of the Tower this morning for the Queen's trial. I did not want to be there, but Mama was determined to go. She still blames Anne for the ruining of Catherine's marriage, and said she wanted to see justice done. I was not sure if one could call the proceedings justice, but I could not refuse her. I certainly would not let her fight her way through those crowds on her own.

Men must have been working through the whole weekend to put up the central platform and the tiers of benches that surrounded it. At least 2,000 people were crammed into the place, all of them as agog with excitement as though they were at a circus. The Duke of Norfolk sat on a throne under a grand canopy, for he represented the Crown. King Henry was not present, and neither was Jane Seymour. Chairs were provided for the 26 peers who were to judge Anne's case. The chief executioner stood at the entrance, holding his axe between his feet. Its blade was turned away, to show that Anne was not yet condemned.

I had been afraid they might have to assist her in, weeping and trembling, but Anne made her entrance with great dignity. She curtsied to the judges, and stared round at the assembled crowd as though she found it fascinating that so many people were present. Then she moved to the chair in the centre of the platform, and seated herself on it with complete composure.

The long list of charges was read out, and after each one Anne declared her innocence. She spoke clearly and firmly, and people were impressed. In the murmur that followed one of her statements, I heard a man behind me say, "She will see them off yet." I turned to look at him, but his companion was smiling grimly. "No chance," he said. "They have to condemn her. The King wishes it. And Cromwell stands to lose his own head if the Queen walks out of here a free woman."

All 26 of the noblemen declared her guilty. Anne still held her head high, as though she had faced the fact already, and conquered her fear. The Duke of Norfolk, on the other hand, cracked at the last moment. When he stood to pronounce the sentence his voice shook and tears were in his eyes. After all, Anne is his sister's child. The words he spoke have imprinted themselves on my mind:

Because thou hast offended our sovereign lord the King's Grace in committing treason against his person, the law of the realm is this: that thou shall be burnt here within the Tower of London on the Green, else to have thy head smitten off, as the King's pleasure shall be further known of the same.

There was an instant outbreak of talking and one or two people cheered, but louder than all the noise was a terrible scream from somewhere high in the tiered seats. There was a commotion up there, people trying to support a woman who had collapsed. I learned afterwards that it was Mrs Orchard, Anne's old nurse.

The Queen waited for the hubbub to be hushed, then she spoke. I will set down her words, too, as well as I remember them. She began by saying she had been condemned for reasons very different from the ones given. Nobody dared to nod agreement, though we all knew she was right. She went on to speak of the King:

I do not say I have always shown him that humility which his goodness to me merited. I confess I have had jealous fancies and suspicions of him, which I had not discretion enough, and wisdom, to conceal. But God knows, and is my witness, that I have not sinned against him in any other way.

She said that she was not trying to prolong her life. "God hath taught me how to die," she said, "and He will strengthen my faith." She spoke sadly of her brother and the other "unjustly condemned" men, and said she would willingly suffer many deaths to deliver them. Her last words were very brave:

Since I see it pleases the King, I shall willingly accompany them in death, with this assurance, that I shall lead an endless life with them in peace.

She turned and left the hall then, walking between two ladies. The Chief Executioner now held his axe with the sharp edge of its blade turned towards her.

They found her brother guilty as well. The only evidence against him was that of his own wife. Everyone knows she hates him, so we thought he might be acquitted. He spoke fluently in his own defence, and things seemed to be going well for him, but then he was handed a piece of paper. He read the words written on it and frowned as if perplexed. A flush of embarrassment came over his face.

One of the lords said, "The paper is a statement allegedly made by yourself. Would you care to read it out?"

Rochford shook his head. "I cannot—" He halted, then began again. He was stumbling over his words, and I hardly caught what he was saying. "Create suspicion ... prejudice the issue the King might have from a second marriage..."

The court burst into uproar. I turned to Mama and asked, "What does it mean?"

"That the King is impotent, and will have no more children with any woman," she said as the roars of outrage went on. "And if he wrote the words on that paper, he is a dead man, for they are high treason."

Rochford had just realized the same thing. "I did not say it!" he shouted, though his voice was drowned in the continuing rumpus. "I did not say it!"

I am sure he spoke the truth, and he had not written the words on the paper they handed him, but it was too late. The trick had worked, and Rochford was condemned. His death is to be the same terrible one that awaits Mark and the others.

The King is holding a river pageant as I write this, in celebration of his coming freedom from Anne. The palace servants started work a week ago to get everything ready, so he must have been very sure she would be found guilty.

I went down to the kitchen to talk to William, and he was with a giggling crowd of cooks surrounding one of them who was singing a scurrilous ballad about Jane Seymour. I had heard something similar being sung in the streets as Mama and I came back from the Tower. Londoners are enjoying themselves at the expense of Henry and his new woman.

I joined in the laughter, I must admit. Dreadful though it all is, the jester in me finds a rich comedy in the King's dealings with his royal wives. This evening though, I cannot help thinking of poor Anne, waiting to hear if she is to die by the fire or the axe. I hope, for her sake, Henry chooses the latter – it is more merciful.

16th May 1536

Anne has asked that her little niece, Katherine Carey, shall be sent to keep her company in these last days. The child is only seven years old. I would not like a daughter of mine to do such a thing. I can only hope little Katherine does not understand too much of what is to happen.

Cranmer was with the Queen this morning, they say because the King wants a divorce before she dies. I could not see why Anne should grant him such a request – it seemed no more than a last humiliation. But rumour has it that Cranmer told her she might be reprieved if she agreed to it, so she did so with great gladness.

I wonder if the King really means to pardon her? He seems to be of more generous mind now his plan has succeeded. He has amended the dreadful penalty on Mark, Rochford and the others, God be thanked. They will still die, but simply by the headsman's axe, with none of the grisly torture that had been planned. They will be executed tomorrow.

17th May 1536

Anne had to watch the five men die. She was taken to different quarters in the Tower this morning, with a window overlooking the Green and its straw-covered platform. Her brother made a long, brave speech to the watching crowd, they say, and all the men swore that both they and the Queen were innocent. Mark was the last to die. It must have been terrible for him, because the scaffold was awash with blood by then. He made no speech. He just asked the people to pray for him, and said he deserved death. We will never know the truth of what happened now. God rest his soul.

Anne's marriage to Henry was declared invalid today. I see now why the King wanted a divorce. Anne's little daughter, Elizabeth, becomes illegitimate once her mother's marriage to her father is broken. The same is true of Mary, the daughter of Catherine. With neither of the girls recognized as a rightful heir, the way is now clear for a child of Jane Seymour's to inherit the throne.

Henry has chosen to have his former wife beheaded rather than burned. He has sent to France for a skilled swordsman who guarantees to sever a neck with a single blow.

18th May 1536

The swordsman is not here yet because he was delayed on the road from Dover. A man who came here with a message for the King told us the Queen was distressed to hear of the delay. The execution was set for this morning, and she had hoped it would be over by now. The man said the Constable of the Tower assured her there would be no pain, and she laughed and put both hands round her slender throat, saying she had only a little neck.

I wish I did not have to hear such details. Like everyone else, I have seen many executions, and always thought nothing of them, but it is different when I know the condemned prisoner so well. I might have been in her place, had our paths followed different ways. I cannot stop thinking about her. I keep remembering the moment when she leaned her head towards me in need of comfort. I wish now that I had responded.

Ever since the death sentence, Henry has been behaving with a gaiety that most of us find distasteful. Perhaps he does not want to be alone with his conscience. Whatever the reason, he has plunged into constant parties and celebrations, with musicians playing and much feasting and drinking. I myself have been summoned several times to play for him. I reminded him yesterday that I am officially dismissed, but he just shrugged his heavy shoulders. Music, he said, speaks more sweetly than words.

19th May 1536

It is over. Anne Boleyn, Queen of England, died this morning at nine o'clock. The King did not witness her execution, and neither did the Duke of Norfolk. I was there with Mama. She insisted on seeing the end of "that woman" – for the sake of Queen Catherine, she said. Tom kept the children in the smithy with him. They always like the smoke and the clanging iron and the patient horses.

The time of the execution was supposed to be a secret, but a huge crowd of people had crammed onto the green in the centre of the Tower. The scaffold had been built high, so that everyone could see, and it was draped with black cloth and scattered with straw. The heavy wooden block stood in the centre, with a lot of straw at its base. The executioner wore black clothes, with a hood that covered his head and a mask over his face, as if he was taking part in some grim carnival. There was no sword in his hand, and a man beside me said it was hidden in the pile of straw behind him. He was right – when I looked carefully I could see the hilt sticking out. A priest stood ready, murmuring prayers.

The crowd hushed its chatter as the procession came out onto the green led by Sir William Kingston, the Constable of the Tower. Four ladies followed Anne – the same four who had been watching over her in these last days. The Queen wore a crimson kirtle and a gown of black damask with a low square neck, and her dark hair was bound high about her head, with a French hood over it. Every one of the people present must have been staring at her white neck, as I was myself. I will never forget how pure it looked, and how vulnerable. She kept glancing behind her, as if certain that someone must at any moment come to tell her this thing was not going to happen – that Henry had forgiven her and all was well. It saddened me, for I knew nobody would come.

Anne climbed the steps to the scaffold, followed by her ladies. Although none had been a friend to her, they looked distressed now, and Lady Lee, Thomas Wyatt's sister, was in tears. Anne spoke to them kindly, begging their pardon for any harshness of hers and wishing them happiness in serving their next mistress. Then she turned to the Constable and asked him to give her time to make her last statement. He inclined his head in permission, and she addressed the crowd. She spoke very clearly, again swearing she was innocent of any wrongdoing.

Kingston then gave her a purse containing money for the executioner. It seemed terrible to me that the Queen had to pay the man who was going to kill her. The black-clad man knelt before her, asking pardon for what he had to do, and she handed him the purse with complete composure, as though she were giving alms to the needy. He got to his feet and stepped back, bowing in thanks. Then he retreated to stand by the pile of straw.

Anne gave the prayer book she had been holding to Lady Lee, who wept afresh. The other three ladies helped her take off her necklace and her French hood. They tied a blindfold over Anne's eyes, then assisted her to kneel down. They had to guide her hands so she could locate the block and lower her head across its central ridge.

The whole assembled crowd knelt as well, out of respect, and when the shuffling stilled, we could hear the Queen praying aloud, "Jesus, receive my soul! O Lord God, have pity on my soul! To Christ I commend my soul!" She repeated the words again and again while the executioner quietly took his sword from the straw and came to the block. He raised the blade high, and it fell so fast that we hardly saw the movement.

The black-clad man retrieved the head from where it lay in the straw, and held it up to show the crowd. In his heavy French accent, he pronounced the formal words as best he could, "Zus perish all ze King's enemies." Nobody was listening to him. The lips of the dead Queen were still moving as though her prayer continued, and several people cried out in horror. The Tower guns fired as a signal that the execution had been carried out, and the crowd began to move away, very quietly. There had been no rejoicing for Anne when she was crowned Queen, but neither was there any triumph at her death.

I was in tears. I thought Mama would chide me for my softness over a woman who had done such harm, but she did not. "I have wished for her death many times during these years," she said, "but not on a trumped-up charge that she did not deserve. God have mercy on her soul." And we both made the sign of the cross.

I looked back as we left the green. Anne's four ladies were alone on the scaffold, weeping as they performed the last service for their dead mistress. I watched as they lifted her mutilated body and placed it in the arrow-chest that had stood behind the straw. Lady Lee was sobbing bitterly as she held a white cloth, ready to cover it. I turned away to join Mama, and we went out.

The remains of Anne Boleyn were buried this afternoon in the Tower's Royal Chapel of St Peter ad Vincula.

15th September 1536

This has been one of those golden autumn days, with the sky as blue as Michaelmas daisies. I spread the washed linen over the bushes to dry in the sun, then went with the children to pick brambles for a pie. We asked Mama if she would come, but she did not want to get her fingers pricked by thorns and stained with red juice. Besides, she said, she needed the bright daylight for her work, as her eyes are not what they were. We left her sitting at the cottage door, stitching at the little gown she is making. It is of fine white linen, pin-tucked and with embroidery at the neck and sleeves. It will be so good to have her help when the new baby is born.

The King was betrothed to Jane Seymour on the day following Anne's execution, announcing that he would marry her at the end of May – which he did. He was in high good humour and inclined to be generous, which was lucky for us. He listened with a benevolent smile to our request to leave the court, and made no objection. He even gave us a purse of gold, in recognition of the long service done to him and his family by Mama and Tom and myself, and this has been a godsend to us. We left the court a week after Anne's death.

I am glad now that I was not born a boy, as I wished so often when I was younger. For the time being, I no longer want excitement and change. I find tremendous pleasure in my children and in the task of making this tumbledown cottage into a warm home. The daily work is hard, but Tom and I share it between us, and Daniel's strength and enthusiasm is a big help. He is eighteen now, well able to take on the heavier tasks. Tom bought a horse last week, a good cob mare, six years old. The children call her Bessie. She is strong and good-natured, and as I write this I can hear Tom hammering at the plough he is making. Over the winter we can break a lot of new ground, ready to sow wheat and barley for the coming year, and more vegetables.

There are only a few pages left in this diary now, and I will keep them for special days in our family life. I pray that the King may be happy with Jane. I hope she will give him the son he wants, for only then will the fears and suspicions that fill this poor country be hushed.

May the soul of Anne Boleyn, who at the end was so brave and so undeserving of her fate, rest in peace.

Historical Note

The date of Anne Boleyn's birth is not known, but it was probably around 1501–2. Some historians suggest a later date of around 1507, but this would only make her six years old when she entered court service, which seems unlikely. Anne's mother had royal connections, being the daughter of the Earl of Surrey, but her father was an undistinguished Norfolk tradesman. However, he gave his four children a good education, and Anne wrote in a beautiful hand, spoke good French and was skilled at music and embroidery. In 1513 she was sent to serve as a court lady to Margaret of Austria, Regent of the Netherlands.

The following year Mary Tudor, sister of Henry VIII, was betrothed to Louis XII, the King of France, and Anne Boleyn became one of her maids of honour. Anne's elder sister, also called Mary, was at this French court as well. When war was threatened between England and France in 1522, the royal betrothal fell through and the girls returned to London, where Mary Boleyn was briefly King Henry's mistress. When he tired of Mary, Henry's interest turned to the younger sister, but Anne already had a suitor, Henry Percy. The King ordered Wolsey to dismiss Percy from court. Anne was furious, and said so, for she never learned the wisdom of holding her tongue. She, too, was dismissed for her cheekiness, and spent a year with her parents at Hever Castle in Kent. She returned to court in 1524 or 1525, where she served the Queen, Catherine of Aragon, wife of Henry VIII since 1509.

Catherine, daughter of Queen Isabella of Spain, had previously married Henry's elder brother, Arthur, in 1501, but Arthur had died only six months later. This led to a long debate between various political factions as to whether her subsequent marriage to Henry was legal or not. Catherine adored her husband, but trouble arose between them because they had only one child, Mary, who would become Mary I of England. Henry desperately wanted a male heir, and his desire for a son made him impatient with Catherine. He had set his heart on a new, younger wife, and by 1526 he was wildly in love with Anne Boleyn. Anne was ambitious and clever, and she had seen from her sister's example that the King's favours could be short-lived, so she kept Henry at arm's length. This astonished him, and increased his determination to marry her.

In Catholic England divorce was unheard of, but Henry found a passage in the Bible stating that marriage between a man and his dead brother's wife was illegal in the sight of God. A long wrangle with the Church in Rome began on this point, and the whole case became known as "The King's great matter".

Anne's uncle, the Earl of Norfolk, saw that his family could gain immense power in the court if his niece should become queen, so he and his supporters were strongly in favour of Henry's divorce from Catherine. Cardinal Wolsey, the King's closest adviser but also the Pope's representative of the Church, opposed this. Anne hated Wolsey, and in 1530 she persuaded Henry to have him arrested for treason. Wolsey died the same year, on his way to imprisonment in the Tower.

The Pope dithered and would give no judgement on the "great matter", being fearful of offending other powerful rulers, notably Catherine's nephew, the Emperor Charles, who dominated most of Europe. Henry was exasperated by the endless delays and began to lose all respect for the authority of Rome. In 1531 he separated from Catherine, sending her away to live in first one house then another, each a little smaller and less pleasant than the last.

In 1532 Henry granted Anne a peerage in her own right. Anne was not popular with the people, but she began openly to plan for her marriage to the King. Early in 1533 she became pregnant.

Although he had still not divorced his first wife, Henry married Anne in a secret ceremony within a few weeks of knowing she expected a child. The Pope threatened to excommunicate him, but by now Henry was planning with Archbishop Cranmer to establish a separate Church that would be answerable only to the reigning monarch of England, and not to Rome.

On Easter Sunday 1533 he paraded Anne through the streets of London as his chosen consort, but Catherine continued to insist that she, and only she, was England's crowned queen. The common people agreed with this, and resented Henry's infidelity to his faithful wife. Anne, conversely, was greeted with catcalls from the crowds wherever she went. A few weeks later, Cranmer took on himself the authority to judge the King's case, and declared Henry's marriage to Catherine null and void. With this final break from Rome, the Church of England was born – and Henry could consider himself a free man.

Anne Boleyn was crowned on 1 June 1533. On 7 September of that year, she gave birth, not to the longed-for son but to a girl, Elizabeth, who would become Queen Elizabeth I of England. None of her subsequent babies survived. Modern medical opinion suggests that Anne may have been rhesus negative, meaning that no child of hers after the first one could tolerate the type of blood circulating in its system. In our own time, such babies can be saved through blood transfusion, but for the Tudors, the condition was mysterious and fatal. Henry began to tire of his new wife, who was proving no more capable of providing a son than the discarded Catherine.

The three brief years of Anne Boleyn's marriage saw Henry's love for her turn to loathing. He began to look elsewhere, and in 1535 he fell in love with the meek and submissive Jane Seymour. However, with two wives still living, another divorce was out of the question. Abetted by his new adviser, Thomas Cromwell, Henry began to think of a more drastic solution.

On 7 January 1536 Catherine of Aragon died. Henry showed no great regret.

On the night following Catherine's funeral Anne Boleyn lost the baby she had been expecting. For Henry this was the last straw, and he raged that she should have no more children by him. Just over three months later a court was appointed to investigate charges that Anne had committed treason against the King by having illicit relationships with several other men, one of them her own brother. She was arrested and taken to the Tower of London.

At her trial Anne swore she was innocent of the charges. Her eloquence moved many people, but it could not save her. Both she and the men accused with her were sentenced to die. Anne Boleyn was beheaded on Tower Green at nine o'clock in the morning of Friday 19 May 1536. Henry VIII announced his betrothal to Jane Seymour the next day, and married her the following month, on 30 June.

In 1537 Jane gave birth to a boy, Edward, but she died of childbirth fever a few days later.

Henry subsequently married Anne of Cleves, then Catherine Howard, and lastly Catherine Parr, to whom he was still married when he died in 1547. None of these wives gave him any further children, and Henry was succeeded by his nine-year-old son, Edward VI. The six years of the boy's reign ended with his death in 1553. Catherine of Aragon's daughter, Mary, became queen, but she died after only five years, in 1558.

Anne Boleyn's daughter, Elizabeth, then came to the throne and ruled wisely and magnificently for 45 years. Perhaps in abiding fear of the fate that had overtaken her mother, she never married, and the Tudor dynasty came to an end with her death in 1603.

Timeline

1491 Henry VIII is born as Prince Henry, son of the first Tudor king, Henry VII.

1501 Prince Henry's older brother, Arthur, marries Catherine of Aragon.

In the same year or the next, Anne Boleyn is born.

1502 Arthur dies.

1509 Henry VII dies.

Prince Henry is crowned King Henry VIII, and marries Catherine of Aragon.

1513 Anne Boleyn is sent to serve at the French court of Mary Tudor, who is betrothed to Louis XII of France.

1516 Catherine of Aragon has a daughter, Mary, later to be Queen Mary I.

1522 War is threatened between England and France, and Mary Tudor's betrothal ends.

Anne Boleyn returns to England and enters the court of Henry VIII.

1523 Henry Percy wants to marry Anne Boleyn, but the engagement is forbidden by Wolsey, at the insistence of Henry VIII. Anne is banished to her parents' home, Hever Castle.

1524 Anne Boleyn returns to court, in the service of Catherine of Aragon.

1525 Henry VIII begins to tire of Catherine, who has failed to give him a male heir and is unlikely to have any more children. He falls in love with Anne Boleyn, and plans to seek a divorce from Catherine.

1526 "The King's great matter" about his divorce begins. Divorce is illegal within Catholic England, but Anne Boleyn has powerful allies. The Pope fails to give judgement.

1530 Anne Boleyn persuades Henry VIII to arrest Cardinal Wolsey for treason. Wolsey dies on his way to imprisonment in the Tower of London.

1531 Henry VIII separates from Catherine of Aragon.

1532 Henry grants a peerage to Anne Boleyn. Archbishop Cranmer advises him that the "great matter" may be decided by the King and the English clerics, without reference to the authority of Rome.

1533 Anne Boleyn becomes pregnant, and Henry VIII marries her secretly, although he is still married to Catherine of Aragon. Following a judgement from Cranmer, Henry divorces Catherine, and the Protestant Church of England is established.

Anne Boleyn is crowned Queen of England, and on 7 September gives birth to a daughter, Elizabeth, later to be Queen Elizabeth I.

1534 Anne Boleyn's next baby is still-born. Relationships between her and Henry VIII begin to deteriorate.

1535 Henry VIII falls in love with Jane Seymour, and seeks to free himself from Anne Boleyn, who fails to give him a son.

1536 Catherine of Aragon dies.

Anne Boleyn suffers another miscarriage.

Henry appoints a court to judge Anne on charges of adultery with several other men, including her own brother. She pleads innocence, but is condemned to death.

On 19 May Anne Boleyn is beheaded at the Tower of London.

Henry VIII announces his betrothal to Jane Seymour, and marries her on 30 June.

1537 Jane Seymour dies after giving birth to a son, Edward, later to be Edward VI.

1540 Henry VIII marries Anne of Cleves, but divorces her the same year.

He marries Catherine Howard.

1541 Catherine Howard is beheaded.

1542 Henry marries Catherine Parr.

1547 Henry VIII dies.

Henry's son by Jane Seymour is crowned Edward VI, at the age of nine.

1553 Edward VI dies.

Catherine of Aragon's daughter is crowned Queen Mary I.

1558 Mary dies.

Anne Boleyn's daughter, Elizabeth I, comes to the throne and rules for 45 years. She never marries.

1603 Elizabeth I dies and the Tudor dynasty ends.

A portrait of Henry VIII by Hans Holbein the Younger.

A portrait of Anne Boleyn by an unknown artist. Anne wears a necklace with a gold "B" and three pearl pendants.

A view of Hampton Court at the time it was first built.

A modern illustration of Henry VIII visiting Hever Castle, a family home of Anne Boleyn.

A chalk portrait of Thomas Cromwell by Hans Holbein the Younger.

An engraving of Cardinal Wolsey, Henry VIII's adviser.

An illustration showing a jousting tournament. Jousting is a sport where mounted knights attempt to knock each other off their horses using lances. Jousting was one of Henry VIII's favourite pastimes.

An engraved portrait of Jane Seymour, Henry VIII's third wife.

Picture acknowledgments

P 248   Henry VIII, Thyssen-Bornemisza Collection, Madrid, Spain/Bridgeman Art Library

P 249   Anne Boleyn, Mary Evans Picture Library

P 250   Hampton Court, Mary Evans Picture Library

P 251   Henry VIII at Hever Castle, Mary Evans Picture Library

P 252   Thomas Cromwell, Collection of the Earl of Pembroke, Wilton House, Wilts,UK/Bridgeman Art Library

P 252   Cardinal Wolsey, Mary Evans Picture Library

P 253   Jousting, Private Collection/Bridgeman Art Library

P 254   Jane Seymour, Mary Evans Picture Library

My Story.